To Sketch a Sphinx

More from Phase Publishing
by

Rebecca Connolly

The Arrangements

An Arrangement of Sorts

Married to the Marquess

Secrets of a Spinster

The Spinster Chronicles

The Merry Lives of Spinsters

The Spinster and I

Spinster and Spice

The London League

The Lady and the Gent

A Rogue About Town

A Tip of the Cap

By Hook or By Rook

Fall from Grace

To Sketch a Sphinx

Rebecca Connolly

Phase Publishing, LLC
Seattle

Cover art by Tugboat Design
http://www.tugboatdesign.net

Phase Publishing, LLC first paperback edition
August 2020

ISBN 978-1-952103-13-1
Library of Congress Control Number 2020912428
Cataloging-in-Publication Data on file.

Acknowledgements

To the London League for being the best bunch of guys to write about, and starting me on this fantastic spy journey, which may never end. Y'all are my favorites, and no one of you is more favorite than another. I promise.

And to opera and peanut M&Ms, the combination of which made this story infinitely better for many reasons.

Chapter One
London, 1825

"Hal! Hal, where are you?"

Hal chose not to answer. Couldn't answer. Not now, not in the middle of this project.

"Sir, as I said…" Thad's gravelly, barely polite voice was full of exasperation, and yet tinged with respect.

How odd.

"Hal! HAL!"

"Sir…"

The door creaked open loudly. "Hal, are you home?"

"Would you have been let in if I were not?"

"You know, that is a remarkably excellent question."

"I do make it a point to have those when I can."

Silence reigned, and Hal wondered if the voice bellowing throughout the house had actually heard that last statement, muttered as it had been.

The only sound for some moments was that of charcoal gliding against paper, the tone shifting and moving with each new angle and avenue. The face was beginning to come to life, shapes transforming into features, imitation morphing into reflection, and the thrill of excitement that came with the witnessing of that change began to rise.

Almost. Almost.

"Ah, there you are!"

The charcoal stopped moving, and Hal exhaled a short sigh

before turning to glance at the tall man now leaning in the doorway of the makeshift study.

"Where did you expect me to be?" she asked.

The man grinned, though the charming appearance of it would have no effect here. "I gather there are a limited number of locations I could have chosen from?"

Hal lifted a brow and attempted to return to the drawing. "I am only ever in two places at home, Weaver. Here or my bedchamber. As it is not early morning or the middle of the night, it is only right that I should be here in my study."

"You call this a study? Surely, a gallery or a library would be more appropriate. Or… a drawing room, as it were."

The charcoal stopped once more, and Hal glared at the guest. "That was poorly done. Thad could do better."

Weaver shrugged easily, still grinning. "I don't know, I thought it was rather witty."

"No."

"Oh well. Perhaps next time."

Sighing, Hal set down the charcoal in earnest and pushed her spectacles atop her loosely pinned curls. "Is there something I can do for you, Weaver? Or were you hoping for a social call?"

Weaver pushed into the room and waved dismissively. "No, no, I understand and appreciate your spite for all social endeavors. And I know full well that if I were to come on any matter other than business, I would have to bring my wife, or else I would be barred from the house."

"Too right," Hal grunted, shifting on her settee as Weaver took a seat in the nearby wingback chair. "Though you know full well she could never be seen calling here. I'm supposed to be living in shame, remember?"

"Indeed," came Weaver's reply with the accompanying sage nod. "Your family discredited and all that. I do hope you are bearing up the burden as best you can."

Hal finally managed to flick a rueful smile at the sarcasm. "I manage well enough. Such a pity to not have more respectable friends."

Weaver smiled very blandly. "Yes, I can see that you feel the loss keenly."

"Quite." She batted her lashes once, then snorted and looked down at the portrait, frowning slightly.

Something was off. Her eyes darted here and there, looking for what was missing or wrong. She had felt so in tune with her memory, so detailed in her recollection, but now…

"And what are we working on at the present?"

Hal glanced up at Weaver, who was watching her with an interest that she did not trust at all. She had worked with him for years, at least a full decade, and when he had an idea or a plan, his expression tended to resemble a cat happening upon a particularly plump and unsuspecting mouse. However, this cat wielded incomparable political power and influence, and he could take down any number of monarchies with his wealth of information if he had chosen to do so.

Which, naturally, Weaver would never do.

Anymore.

"It's supposed to be what I remember of my mother," Hal admitted without any hint of sentimentality, for she had none where her mother was concerned.

Weaver raised a questioning brow. "But you have portraits, surely."

"In the family home," she confirmed with a quick nod. "At my brother's estate, naturally. Here? Not a one. As it really is too much trouble to send for one, considering, I thought I would do what I could from memory."

"I would say such a thing would be extraordinarily difficult, given the passage of time, but with your gifts, I can only say that I wonder at your struggling with it." He smiled with a surprising degree of warmth. "She was an extraordinary woman."

Hal made a face and returned to her drawing, looking for the error she would need to correct. "Some would say that, yes. I doubt you will hear my brother or myself say any such thing."

"You don't know what she was involved in," Weaver warned with some firmness. "You don't know the details."

"And despite our asking, those questions have yet to produce any sort of satisfactory answer." She glanced over at him with a pointed look.

He met it without shame. "You both know why. Your father knew why."

Hal nodded and plastered a false smile on her face. "I have no doubt Father knew more than we ever did. I understand the secrecy, Weaver, having lived my entire life with it, but to have never known one's mother in truth is particularly cruel."

"She was every bit as you knew her," Weaver assured her with more gentleness than she had ever heard from him. "I can promise you that."

"But where did her loyalty lie?" Hal murmured, shocking herself with the pain that she felt suddenly rising to the surface. She cleared her throat quickly and set the sketch aside entirely. "It doesn't matter. My memories of her are limited as it is, and I likely cannot trust a memory from childhood to be accurate."

Weaver made a soft, noncommittal sound. "I think you could trust your memory from the moment you were born, my dear."

She only shrugged and folded her legs up beneath her. "You said this was business. As you are here yourself, may I assume this is not tied to the League? Or, indeed, to any particular office?"

"You may," he confirmed as he straightened in his chair. "What I have… what we need transcends any group or mission."

Hal's brows shot up at that. She had never been approached with such a severe tone, or with such a prospect. She was a well-known and well-used asset to every office with covert operations, had participated in meetings and debriefings with some of the most dangerous individuals Britain could boast, and even some from other shores. She would have been an operative herself had she any skill with combat and self-defense, but she had made herself useful regardless.

Everything from the Shopkeepers, the highest officers in covert operations, had specific responsibilities and missions. Everything she ever did for them was strategically assigned. To have an assignment without any of that was unusual, if not unheard of.

"Trick?" she asked with some alarm, her thoughts instantly shifting to her brother, her twin, who was presently undercover yet again, so much so that he wasn't able to even write. He was nearly always on a mission, but he was usually able to send her word with some regularity.

Not this time.

Not this mission.

Weaver shook his head firmly, allowing himself to smile. "No, he is well, as of his last reporting. Quite well, as it happens."

Hal breathed a tiny sigh of relief. Hunter wasn't reckless or careless, but he did tend to get himself into quite a bit of danger, which never got easier for her. She seldom knew the details of his missions, which was for the best, but every now and then, she could figure a thing or two out.

The world thought he was a hopeless reprobate who had ruined the family and their legacy, not to mention any chances for a good match for his sister; the truth was anything but.

Neither Hal nor Hunter cared. Their lives had been upended with the death of both parents in the space of two years just as Hunter had been sent away to school. They had no family but each other, and there wasn't much they cared for other than that.

Apart from England herself.

"So what is it, then?" Hal inquired, once her heart had settled back into its place. "Forgeries? Maps? Composite sketches? I've gotten quite good at certificates of death, if any of those are needed."

"I feel more like a criminal every time I visit you," Weaver grumbled good-naturedly. "No to all of that. This is something quite particular, and yet incredibly vague."

Hal frowned at him. "That doesn't make any sense to me, Weaver."

His sheepish look worried her. "It will in a minute." He sobered, then exhaled. "We need you to come on assignment. As an agent, not only an asset."

"Out in the field?" Hal blinked and shook her head. "I'm not qualified for the field, Weaver. I have no doubt you have seen my file, which explains everything."

"You studied at Miss Masters, did you not?" he asked without any note of concern. "And in the specialized program?"

Hal flicked her fingers in an obvious gesture. "Of course I did, you know that."

Weaver gave her a firm nod. "Then you have all the preparation you will need. We've even given you a code name. How do you feel about being called Sketch?"

"I was pathetic in combat training," Hal reminded him, ignoring the mention of a code name as she sat forward, almost straining towards him. "Those are not my words. That is how Fists described me. 'Pathetic. Lacking all coordination, notably weak on the left side, shows no aptitude for any weapon at all, and hopeless at defending herself from attack. Most likely to die within the first minute of any assault.' "

The lordly man before her only stared, clearly calling upon his more diplomatic skill set to avoid any reaction to her words. Then he shook his head slowly. "That memory of yours, Hal. By Jove, it's a wonder."

She snorted softly. "You don't need a memory like mine to remember something like that, Weaver."

He tilted his head to one side. "How did you see the report? Those are supposed to be classified."

She only looked back at him with a flat smile.

"At any rate," he went on, overriding her lack of answer smoothly, "that makes little difference here, because there will be no fighting at all. Not in the physical sense, anyway."

"I will pretend that you are making sense in hopes that your point will soon be clear," Hal remarked dryly.

Weaver raised a brow. "We need you to accompany another of our assets on a mission into France. Paris, to be precise."

A startled cough escaped Hal, and she barely managed to recover herself enough to look apologetic about doing so.

"Oh," she coughed again. "Is that all?"

He gave her a brisk nod. "The pair of you will infiltrate Society there and find every opportunity to discover what you can of the Faction. Its leaders, its sympathizers, its plans…"

"Surely, you have operatives in France, Weaver," Hal protested, the tips of her fingers beginning to tingle.

"We do." He dipped his chin in acknowledgement. "They will be your contacts, as well as your informants. But due to the nature of their missions, they cannot break away from their current assignments for this task."

There was something unsettling about that notion, that those with more skills and information, let alone connections, could not be bothered to do what was being asked of her. Was that due to the danger of the assignment being posed to her or due to a sense that this was not nearly as important as Weaver was making it out to be?

"I can see your mind spinning. Ask what you must."

Hal brought her eyes back to Weaver's, not entirely realizing she had ever looked away. She fought a frown as she looked at him. This man had been like an uncle to her for most of her life, had been somehow a godfather and mentor throughout, and likely knew her better than any other person apart from her twin. He already knew what she wanted to know, but he was just maddening enough to keep everything to himself apart from what she would ask.

Always secrets, always partial information. Never the full truth.

Which was well enough, as he did not have her full truth, either.

"Why?" she asked without any sort of tact.

His mouth quirked to one side. "You know better than that. More specific, please."

It had been worth a try, and Hal had to smile at being so neatly caught. "Why me? Why not them? Why now?"

Weaver nodded at each of the questions and crossed his leg over one knee, his fingers lacing atop them. "Why, indeed. We need you because of those maddening skills we've already discussed, as well as the artistry of your fingers. We need exact information that can be trusted without question, and you are the perfect person to manage that."

She'd rather expected something of that nature, so that was no surprise.

"Why not them?" Weaver repeated, moving on. "We cannot trust in the safety of our operatives with something like this. You know about Rogue's potential compromise, and having Trace back in our ranks, though wonderful, poses new risks, as well as new questions. And now, with missing the clerk from the League, as well… How can some of our best operatives be known to our enemies in such a way? We have no idea how many others might face the same. The only viable alternative for this is to send in a team we can guarantee is unknown to all."

That, unfortunately, made a great deal of sense. Her own brother was one of the more dangerous operatives the Crown had and could have any number of threats facing him at any given time. Would she really risk him against those odds when there were none against herself?

She swallowed and nodded at the answer. "And the third?"

Weaver shifted in his chair. "Why now?"

She nodded once more.

He exhaled roughly. "Because I am damned tired of being a step and a half behind in all this, and ready to see us coming against the Faction from a position of strength rather than desperation. Aren't you?"

The question took Hal by surprise. She wasn't among the ranks, anyone would have said so, even if she was a favorite connection of several operatives and their superiors. She had a part to play in the security of England and her interests, it was true, but it had never been a particularly active one.

Her own motivations had never really been considered, even by herself.

But she had seen Trace return only a few weeks ago, and the emotion of that reunion had been significant. She had been curious about the disappearance of One, the longstanding clerk to the London League. She had devoured her brother's letters to her with eagerness, trying to root out any code he might have left therein. She was vastly well protected, and not just because of her brother or her parents. She knew too much, and it was in England's best interest that she remain safe and hidden away as she was.

What was her motivation? What did any of this bring her?

Sad to say, she had no answer. It had simply been what she had always done. Her brother was the one with a rich vein of patriotism and loyalty running through him with all the luster of copper. She had quite simply never thought about the thing long enough to consider anything else.

Only she did know on which side of the line she stood. She knew which flag would fly among the banners of her heart. She couldn't pretend that the idea of actually doing something, physically giving of herself, would not be a relief, given what the rest of her family had willingly endured.

She had felt so pale in comparison to the glorious picture of the rest.

No matter how foolishly they had behaved.

The Mortimer family had given their all; now she would join the ranks. Henrietta Mortimer would finally have the chance to do some good.

The weakest thrill of hope flashed within her, a rather dull sensation, all things considered. She could only hope that her body would have more noteworthy physical responses to such nobility of thought in the future. After much practice, no doubt.

"What would you have me do?" Hal inquired with a tilt of her head. "And when shall I begin?"

Weaver smiled broadly and leaned forward, clasping his hands loosely. "I would have you be the most disgruntled version of yourself in the most refined ways while you and your partner prance about Paris in whatever circles you can manage. There is nothing they would love so much as a British *émigré*."

Hal dipped her chin, her thoughts flying over possibilities. "My mother has cousins in Paris. I could prevail upon them to be my hosts. They are a rare branch of old French nobility that miraculously managed to keep their heads during the Revolution. Literally. No appendages were severed in the maintaining of this family."

"Oh, indeed?" Weaver smiled with satisfaction. "Which family?"

"I haven't the faintest idea." Hal returned his smile with a bland one of her own. "Mother never spoke of it, for obvious reasons. No idea if the cousin I'm thinking of was a *comte,* a *vicomte,* a *marquis*, or simply one of the *petite noblesse.* All I know is he and his wife were very good at aligning themselves most conveniently for the times at hand."

Weaver raised a brow. "Evidently. And what might persuade this family, of which you know so very little, to accept you as a guest with so muddled a connection?"

Hal reached out and patted his hands. "As my superior, I shall rely on your years of diplomatic and covert experience to find a most convincing reason to encourage them. No doubt you have some rather lofty connections of your own to boast."

"One or two," he allowed as he eased back into his chair, eyeing her with some speculation. "The names of your family?"

"De Rouvroy." Hal screwed up her face in thought. "And I'm sorry, I cannot recall if he is the direct descendent or his wife."

Weaver waved that off without concern. "Never you mind, I can unravel the knots of the lineage and peerage, even with Napoleon restructuring of it all." He smiled and rose from his seat. "Thank you for your hospitality, Hal. I will see you soon." He nodded and turned to leave the room.

Hal shot to her feet, following. "Fritz!"

He turned, smiling like the godfather she had always known at the use of his true name. "Henrietta?"

She winced playfully, then tucked a stray curl behind her ear. "You never told me when I will start."

"Did I not?" His smile turned tight and almost formal. "I will need you to come to my home tomorrow evening, just after dark. We'll have a brief rendezvous and go over the details, and then the wedding and you'll be off."

Hal had been in the process of nodding when his words reached her comprehension and she jerked. "Wedding? What wedding?"

Weaver blinked once. "Yours, Hal. Your partner is a man, and we cannot have the pair of you travelling unaccompanied without that protection."

"We're falsifying everything else, why not that?" she demanded, color seeping from her face and leaving a cold vacancy behind.

He heaved a sigh, and for the first time, she could see signs of weariness in him. "Come to my home tomorrow, Hal. I promise, I will explain everything." He smiled again, then left, only the sound of badly squeaking hinges leaving any indication that he had done so.

What had she gotten herself into?

Chapter Two

John Pratt was a sensible man. An intelligent man. Remarkably so, as any number of people would have agreed. He was respectful, respectable, and reliable, all of them to a fault, according to his younger brother. But even he had to pause at the revelation that he would be marrying his partner for this assignment before it could begin in earnest.

Whomever she would be.

Weaver hadn't thoroughly explained himself when he'd come to John with the proposal, and answers hadn't been given then. Only his attendance at the meeting today would grant him those, which was a cruel incentive indeed. The plan for the mission had intrigued John, limited though his information at this stage was. The opportunity to be out in the field, something that had always fallen to his brother's lot, wasn't something that he'd hoped for.

But marrying his partner? What use was it to send in a female spy if they could not do so without the polite expectations or fear of scandal? Surely, there were capable men who were free to make the journey to Paris with him, and who possessed the requisite skills for the task. It would simplify matters easily for both parties and for the superiors they answered to.

Surely, they meant the appearance of a marriage so that the lady in question would be protected from the scandal of jilting, annulment, or divorce from that appearance of a marriage. How exactly they were going to do such a thing was beyond John at the moment, but he made a point not to question the abilities of the Shopkeepers and their associates.

One could never be entirely sure where their intervention had occurred over the history of Britain.

More and more questions swirled themselves about in his head as he stood in this quiet drawing room at the back of Weaver's family home, staring at a painted landscape that could have been done in any county in England. The sort of nondescript rolling hill that he had seen in Hampshire, Shropshire, Derbyshire, and Kent. Was the ambiguity intentional or was the artist quite simply not imaginative enough to find a more distinct subject?

He leaned closer, his eyes narrowing, something about the grass not sitting right with him. The brush strokes were smooth, even, hardly distinguishable from one to the next. But where the ground sloped to the creek, the style and strokes changed, grew rougher, almost clumsy by comparison. Hardly noticeable until it was right before one's eyes, and even then, one had to look.

John was quite used to looking for things that no one else could see. He'd made his life out of it and was well known in certain ranks for it. He had been called a man of riddles and was himself impossible to read. Sphinx had seemed the only name adequate for his code, and he embraced it fully.

He wasn't all that mysterious, in truth. Reserved, observant, and clever. That was all.

More often than not, it sufficed.

With a little time and undivided attention, the most extraordinary things came to life before his eyes, if he could just see the pattern…

"I had no idea you found art so inspiring, Sphinx."

Biting back a scowl, John turned to face the now familiar voice of Weaver, the second in command of all covert operations in England. Weaver was smiling, leaning elegantly against the doorway of the drawing room, looking somewhere between coming in for the day and going out for the evening in his dress. As it was the man's house, it was to be expected, but as John rarely went out for any social occasions, there was only one state of appearance he ever saw on others.

This was not it.

"Care to tell me what it's hiding?" John said with a tilt of his head towards the painting, ignoring the teasing jab.

Weaver smirked and came over to look at it as well. "That one? That is the first landscape my wife painted after the children were born. What makes you think it's hiding something?"

John ran a finger along the area. "Different strokes, not as careful as the rest, layered up."

"Incredible." Weaver shook his head in disbelief. "Nothing nefarious, we didn't purloin it from any dignitary and paint over it. As I said, Emily painted it when the children were quite small. That area, I believe, would have been Alicia's mark when her mother wasn't looking. Rather than start over on a fresh canvas, Emily simply covered it up. Now I have artwork by my wife and my daughter in the same piece. Convenient, eh?"

It was all John could do not to grumble. With all the covert work Weaver had done, both in recent years and in his time before this when he had simply been the Fox, he had fully expected the mystery of the painting to be something worth discussing. The accidental brushstroke of a child was not exactly what he'd had in mind.

"If you say so," John grunted, turning his attention away from the art and strolling to another part of the room. "Who else is coming this evening?"

Weaver went to the sideboard and poured himself some brandy. "Priest and Tailor."

"Tailor is coming himself?" That was a shock, to be sure. Tailor rarely met with operatives in any sort of gathering, communicating more through messages than anything else.

"He insisted," Weaver replied with a firm nod. "Oh, and Sketch, naturally."

John turned to look at him, sliding his hands behind his back. "I'm not familiar with that particular operative. New?"

Weaver's slight smile was unreadable, even for John. "Yes and no."

Never one for the riddle-like manner operatives tended to adopt, John exhaled and flicked two fingers in a weak gesture. "Care to explain?"

Thankfully, Weaver didn't evade further. "She's a new operative, but she is not new to the network."

That limited the list considerably, but not enough to give John any certainty or comfort about his partner. "From the Convent?"

"She is a graduate, yes," Weaver confirmed without hesitation, "and her particular skills will make her an invaluable partner to you."

John grunted softly. "I'll take your word on that."

Weaver was silent for a moment. "Do you have a problem having a woman for your partner in this assignment?" There was an edge to the question that brought John up.

He couldn't start this assignment in the field disgruntled with his superiors, not if he wished to go on assignment ever again.

Provided he'd wish to go on assignment again after this.

There was every chance this could all be a dreadful experience.

"Not in the least," John assured Weaver with a weak attempt at a smile. "I am well aware of how capable and dangerous the ladies of the Convent are. It is only the need for matrimony that I question."

"That would be the question of the evening, would it not?" demanded a sharp, piercing voice that immediately caused the hair on the back of his neck to stand at attention.

It wasn't an unpleasant voice, didn't screech, wouldn't chirp, and resembled nothing at all like the sound of claws on a slate.

It was the identity of the person belonging to that voice that rendered such effects on him.

And suddenly, he felt ill.

Please, Lord, no…

He was praying. He hadn't prayed in a number of years, yet he was praying for deliverance.

He could walk out. He could leave. He hadn't signed anything, hadn't agreed, didn't have to agree, had every right to escape…

"Bloody hell, don't tell me you've paired me with Sphinx, of all people."

John craned his neck from side to side in irritation. "Had to be Hal. Hal is Sketch, Sketch is Hal, doesn't take intellect to make that leap."

"Why is he muttering? What are you muttering over there?"

"Not everything is your business, Hal," John snapped before he could stop himself, turning to glare at the fair-haired tyrant whose hair seemed determined to escape whatever hold she had tamed it into.

Her upper lip curled into a sneer, her pale eyes narrowing. "Listen, Stinks, neither you nor any other pompous…"

"Nice to see you both here," a new voice greeted with a calm steadiness that stopped any argument, though John was still muttering a great deal in his mind.

An older gentleman with a few wrinkles and even fewer strands of hair atop his head entered the room, looking at them both with the sort of familiarity one usually saw in family alone. His gaze started on Hal, and John was pleased to see the woman turn moody and sullen, folding her arms like a temperamental child, though she did obey the silent command.

Then the grey eyes came to John, and the most unnerving sensation of being seen clear through from front to back and every thought and process in between started rising. The impulse to confess a very great deal created the strangest buzzing on his tongue, though John was no great sinner, and his mind began racing all on its own to find some task he had accomplished lately that he could report in on.

Lord Cartwright to the world, and Tailor to those individuals who knew him better, was unquestionably the most powerful man in England. Not even the King himself could cause to happen what this man could, though it would be treason to have expressly said so. Though he was not a man of action at the present, the tales of his exploits as an operative in years past were legendary. Likely exaggerated into the realms of impossible, but no one could quite exclude the possibility.

Not where Tailor was concerned.

A shorter, younger man in the plain ensemble of a clergyman followed, nodding silently and moving to the rear of the room, where he quietly sat and waited.

Priest, John could only assume. He knew little of the man, and even less of the operative, but if the man was legitimately in holy orders…

"The two of you quite understand what you are taking on?" Tailor asked, finally releasing John from the power of his gaze as he set his hat down. "It has been explained to you?"

"Yes," John said at once.

"Not satisfactorily," Hal said at the same time.

John looked at her in exasperation. There was no mistaking the stubbornness in her tone, nor the insolence.

She would get them both killed before they ever reached France purely by her tone.

She met his look with a derisive one of her own. "What? You don't have any more questions on the subject? You're perfectly content to marry me at this minute before we venture off on our assignment?"

Well, when she put it like that…

A shiver raced down his spine and somehow settled in the smallest toe of his right foot. "Perhaps there is a point there," he allowed mildly, turning to face Weaver and Tailor with an apologetic smile.

Tailor, much to his credit, only gave them a faint smile and nodded. "I understand. You comprehend the task of the mission itself?"

"More or less, yes," Hal replied with a much tamer turn of her voice. "Use my mind and my hands, combined with his skill and intellect, to discover who, what, and how regarding the Faction. Yes?"

It was a crudely simple description, but John, for all his attempts, could not find fault in it.

Interesting.

"Yes." Tailor nodded again, just once. "We simply cannot afford to risk more of our valuable operatives to missions associated with the Faction when we have already experienced some compromise with a few. We do not know how secure our connections are any longer, nor how deep the compromise extends. Given the personal connections the pair of you have within the network, that should be motivation enough to succeed, I gather."

John stiffened at the thought of his brother Jeremy being compromised. He'd only just married a few months ago, and to see them in danger already, to potentially have them separated from him for the rest of their lives for protection…

Jeremy was his only family left, and while he might not appear to have any sentiment within a five-mile radius of his person, he was rather attached to that younger brother of his, rascal though he was.

And God help anyone who separated Jeremy from his new wife. Helen would raise hell better than any demon or gorgon possible.

A soft, slow exhale from his left brought John's attention around and he saw, with some interest, Hal bunching her hands into fists at her side and exercising a would-be controlled breath just as he was preparing to do.

It was then he recalled that she also had a brother within the network. Trick, if he recalled, though he had never met him. They'd exchanged correspondence on several occasions, but never met either officially or unofficially. Trick worked alone, which was a risk in and of itself, and was surely in more danger than any two operatives at a time.

What fear and trepidation that must bring to his sister!

The thought wasn't enough to soften his feelings towards Hal, but he would allow for a feeling of sympathy.

However brief.

"There is a file of information," Tailor went on, somehow sensing the renewed dedication in John, at least, if not Hal as well, "that will be made available to you before you sail for France. In it, you will find connections you may avail yourself of during your time in Paris, as well as the most recent and accurate information we can provide you with safely. How you accomplish your tasks will be up to you both, and you will not have a requisite report to make as you progress. Should you have urgent information, you will also have access to a number of avenues to get that information across the Channel and into the proper hands."

He paused, looking them over before smiling to himself. "This is a high Society infiltration, which will require you both to be arrayed as such."

"Oh no…" Hal groaned, shaking her head slowly.

John was not so apprehensive, but he would also claim ignorance.

Weaver snorted once, covering his mouth.

That was never good.

"Tilda, therefore, will be your first stop this evening, once we're done here." Tailor lifted a thick, greying brow. "She will see you suitably outfitted, I believe."

"Undoubtedly," Weaver echoed with a sage nod.

"The costumer?" John prodded, looking between the other two men.

Both nodded. "A valuable asset, I can assure you," Tailor told him firmly, ending any protests or questions John might have countered with next.

A sudden vision of himself dressed as a peacock with a powdered wig and rouge suddenly flashed into his mind, and his enthusiasm began to deflate with every beat of his heart.

"All very well," Hal chimed in, still calmer than before, "I have no quarrel with the task set before us. But why the marriage?"

Tailor and Weaver looked at each other, an unspoken, unreadable message passing between them. "That is purely for respectability," Weaver said slowly, returning his attention to her. "We'll have it annulled when the mission is over. We'll call it fraud, neither of you will suffer for it."

Now it was John whose brows shot up. His personal cover had him working for Bow Street, and so he did, thereby allowing himself some insight into the rule of law and the justice it lived by. Annulments were nigh impossible to obtain, the reasoning behind them equally impossible to prove.

"You want us to marry for respectability, and then get an annulment based on fraud, for respectability?" Hal's question was less incredulous and more dubious.

John could echo the same, though dismay was currently his primary emotion. "Why not make it a marriage in name only?" he asked, forcing his voice to be more restrained than hers.

Tailor's mouth tightened briefly. "Because then you could not get married again, should you wish to."

Hal scoffed loudly. "Because that's likely to happen, isn't it?"

"It's meant to help *you*," Weaver insisted in the most cajoling tone John had ever heard the man employ. "Suppose you get into trouble legally on this mission."

"Why am I the one who failed?" Hal demanded, not at all consoled. "Why not him?"

Her finger jabbing in his direction seemed to actually cause a prodding sensation between his ribs, and his torso tightened in discomfort.

Weaver sighed in resignation. "Look, we're doing this for protection all around. If all goes well, this marriage never took place, and there will be no witnesses to say it did."

"You're killing everyone in this room?" Hal made a point of looking at the rest of the room's occupants. "How ambitious."

John exhaled in irritation and gave her a dark look. "Are you going to be like this for the entire mission?"

She met his eyes squarely. "Probably."

Dipping his chin in acknowledgement, John looked at Tailor. "Do I have to agree in the vows?"

Tailor frowned, then gestured to the quiet man still sitting behind them. "Priest here will see that everything is done properly, and he'll also see that evidence is destroyed properly when the time comes."

Hal folded her arms across her chest, rocking herself up on the balls of her feet, then back down. "And if something goes wrong with that evidence destruction?"

"Then you may have a marriage in name only, and we will set the pair of you up with false identities to start a life somewhere else," Tailor responded with more candor than John expected. "Happy?"

A small smile crossed Hal's lips, rendering her features somehow fairer and yet more feral, her eyes narrowing. "So, you're saying we won't be damned for bigamy. You can arrange that?"

"For heaven's sake, Hal," Weaver groaned as Priest coughed in surprise from his seat.

"What?" Hal inquired with a shrug of her trim shoulders. "I don't want to be kept out of Heaven for the sake of your most convenient arrangement."

Tailor sighed and glanced behind him. "Priest?"

"Tailor?" came the apparently easy answer.

"Can you ensure the state of Hal's immortal soul with regards to this matter?"

The question was a ridiculous one, and John couldn't believe they were indulging her like this. It wasn't an ideal situation for beginning a mission, it was true, and the permanence of the connection might have been in question, but the reasoning was sound, as were the potential ramifications. He wouldn't claim to know much about the Almighty, but surely the value in their mission, and the righteous valor of their assignment, would outweigh any technicality as far as their eternal fate was concerned.

If Hal possessed a spiritual or religious bone in her body, he would be astonished. Knowing that, he could only suspect that she was toying with their superiors and doing all she could to draw this out.

Why, exactly, was less certain, but he was weary with the game already.

"Probably," Priest affirmed with a nod. "I have it on good authority that he is a most forgiving being, and if he allows me to continue to lead part of his flock, with all my missions have required of me, I cannot see him being particularly stringent on this matter."

It was all John could do not to roll his eyes.

Hal seemed almost disgruntled by the statement, which cheered John considerably.

"So?" Weaver pressed with a sigh. "May we proceed?"

John looked at Hal and found Hal looking at him.

He lifted a brow in silent query. She lifted one back, the arch of hers quite perfect in shape and height.

It taunted him more than he would admit.

"Yes," John heard himself say, the admission startling once it was out.

The corner of Hal's lips quirked, and something itched at the corner of John's, though they stayed resolutely where they were.

"We might as well," Hal murmured, turning her attention to the others before them. "A special license, I presume?"

Priest produced the exact license from an inner pocket of his coat. "You presume correctly. And don't worry, I'll cover the cost myself."

"We're covering the cost," Weaver corrected with a roll of his eyes. "The coffers of the government are at your disposal."

Priest grinned, his eyes crinkling. "Even better. I shall send the bill for my services along, as well." He stepped forward, sobering only slightly, and extending his hands out in welcome to the pair of them. "Shall we begin?"

"Hold! I insist you hold!" called a voice from beyond the room.

Hal whirled to face the door, eyes wide. John only looked with mild interest. It was barely a legal marriage and was happening in secret, how could anyone protest it?

A tall man in dark, dirty clothing appeared, his fair hair bared, though just as filthy as the rest of him. He paused at the entry, looking around and beaming quickly. "Am I too late to give the bride away?"

John's brows shot up even as Hal ran to the man and threw her arms around him.

It would seem Trick had arrived.

"You're just in time," Weaver told the newcomer.

Hal whirled to face their superiors, her arm slipping around her brother's waist. "You told him?"

Weaver and Tailor shrugged with eerie synchrony. "Call it a bit of ironic sentimentality."

"I was counselled as to your mission," Trick told his sister, though loud enough for John to hear. "I insisted on having you be protected legally, which is why this marriage is happening. I couldn't possibly let you go through with it without being present myself." He grinned down at her, his teeth almost blinding in their whiteness compared to the dirt that seemed to be everywhere else about him. "It may be the only wedding you have, Hank."

Hal frowned up at him, then surprised the entire room by delivering a stunning right hook to her brother's upper arm. He recoiled with unmasked pain, and John found himself oddly proud of his bride-to-be.

He also made a note to avoid situations where he might receive the same.

"Dammit, Hank," Trick grunted, rolling his shoulder as though testing it. "I've got to work later."

"That is your problem, not mine, Hunt," came the unconcerned reply. She smiled at him with more fondness than John had seen in her expression at any given time.

Despite her harridan-like nature in all else, there was no mistaking her adoration for her brother, nor the closeness between them. Surely, there was something to be said for that.

"Right," Priest said slowly, eyeing the group once more. "It would seem the bride has a suitable escort to give her away, which is hardly what I was most concerned about with this particular wedding. Nevertheless…" He exhaled loudly and gestured to an imagined aisle teasingly. "*Now* shall we begin?"

Chapter Three

"Absolutely not."

"You have to."

"I don't believe I do. Not a required part of the mission in any way, shape, or form."

"You seem to be under the impression that you have any say in the matter, Sphinx. I can assure you, I have been given complete freedom to dress the pair of you as I wish, and what I wish is for you to not stand out on your mission for being such a complete illustration of drudgery and dullness."

Hal snorted a laugh behind her hand as she allowed two of Tilda's girls to take her measurements, glancing over the screen separating her from her new husband as they were fitted for their respective wardrobes. They'd been married all of an hour at most, exchanged only a handful of words beyond their vows, and still he was as surly and fussy as she had ever known him to be.

Granted, their exchanges had all been limited and related to missions they'd both been consulted on. She had no idea how he behaved socially, if he did so at all. She couldn't see him having many social engagements to attend, or indeed being invited to them, given his stoic nature and disinclination to look favorable or pleasing at any moment.

And, at this particular moment, he was protesting rather vigorously to a cravat being tied in a way that can only be described as towering and involved many complicated twists.

It looked ridiculous on him, even she could say that.

"If you could straighten up a bit, miss," the assistant before her asked with all deference. "You're slouching, and I mustn't measure your form that way. It would lead to the most unbecoming fit of gown."

Sobering quickly, Hal did as she was bid, squaring her shoulders and lifting her chin. "Apologies, Belle."

That earned her a smile. "Not at all, miss."

Truth be told, Hal hadn't had to worry about her posture, form, or figure in years. Though she was only twenty-six, which would hardly qualify her to be relegated to the shelf of spinsterdom, she had not gone out in Society for a very long time. Not since Hunter had been seen in a respectable gathering, come to think, as he had publicly been accused of dreadful things that night and the entire family fell into ruin and disgrace.

Not in truth, of course, but it had to be said and done with enough manufactured proof to be believed. As Hunter had been acting the boorish brute for a few years prior in preparation for his role in the covert field, it did not take much for everything to be believed.

Hal was relieved of the duty to engage socially after that, and so she had become every bit the hermit she was rumored to be. She had no friends to speak of and an absent brother her only family.

Except now she had a husband.

In name only, it was true, but still.

The fact sank into the pit of her stomach hard, and she blinked as Belle continued to measure her. A husband, of all things. No wonder Hunter had appeared from the depths of the city to attend the formality. Hal was never supposed to have a wedding or husband of any kind.

Belle suddenly cinched the fabric around Hal's torso tightly, taking her by surprise. "Steady on," Hal protested breathlessly. "What's the point of this?"

"Sorry, miss," Belle said around a mouthful of pins. "Fashions in Paris are starting to turn closer to the body. We'll have to tighten your stays."

Hal's cheeks flamed, and she prayed Sphinx wouldn't hear them.

"Fine," she hissed low to avoid eavesdroppers. "But please, let me breathe. I'll work on comportment, but I must have movement."

The fabric around her loosened just enough to give her breath once more, but only just.

She would take it.

"Tilda, I really must protest," Sphinx insisted, his tone turning plaintive.

"Really? I had no idea," came the tall woman's response.

Hal peered over the top of the screen, her lips curving with curiosity. Sphinx was grimacing, his chin high in the air as Tilda continued to work at the linen about his neck. He wore no waistcoat or jacket, hands propped on his waist, and his stockinged feet curled in abject protest on the floor. It would have been a pitiable picture had this not all felt like some overdone theatrical.

She couldn't laugh at the prospect, much as she was amused by the sight; she knew she would likely have her hair trussed up in a way that would pain her, find herself tripping over the length of her skirts and petticoats, and exposing more of her shoulders and arms than had been seen in a decade.

As if her thought had been heard, the straps of her chemise were drawn to the side, drawing a reluctant groan from her. "Why?"

"Just for estimates, miss," Belle reassured her as the other girl measured the distance between the edges with a strip of fabric. "A glimpse of shoulder is *de rigueur* in Paris."

"I'm beginning to think this is punishment for some crime I have committed," Hal muttered as she obediently spread her arms out when bid.

She heard a grunt from the other side of the screen. "Agreed. Any idea how we have offended the powers that be so heinously?"

Hal smiled and looked towards the ceiling as though it would assist in carrying her voice. "I did manage to forget Tailor's birthday this year until the day after. Think that would do it?"

"Not likely," came the strangely not disparaging voice. "If it had been Weaver, perhaps, but Tailor isn't so vengeful."

"True enough." Hal sighed and made a face. "Could we be receiving punishment on behalf of our siblings, then? Trick and Rook?"

A thoughtful sound emerged. "That could be. I don't know your sibling all that well, but I could certainly see mine causing enough trouble that it could impact me."

"So can I." Hal laughed as she imagined Rook being up to mischief even while on assignment.

"Marvelous," Sphinx replied dryly. "I think everybody can see him doing something."

"I concur," Tilda told them both. "Believe me, both of your brothers are capable of trouble enough to pull the both of you into the mess."

Hal rose up onto her tiptoes to look over the screen at the elegant costumer. "I didn't know you knew Trick."

Tilda glanced over at her with a sly, bemused look. "Oh, love. Believe me, I have known Trick for years and years. I daresay I know more about his missions than you do."

There was a humbling thought, and Hal lowered herself back down as she considered that. She'd known Tilda often helped with several branches of the government's covert operations, but she hadn't suspected anything so incredibly involved. She was a special asset to the London League, of course, but they weren't the only ones running missions and investigations in London itself.

Just how entangled was Tilda in this covert world of theirs?

"May I ask why we are being trussed up like this before we get to Paris?" Sphinx asked Tilda with the same mild, dry tone he always seemed to use. "If I understand things right, we are to be staying with Hal's relations. Surely, they will not expect us to arrive in Paris already arrayed fashionably."

"What are you saying, Sphinx?" Hal demanded with a grin that he wouldn't see. "Are you implying that I am not a fashionable lady?"

Belle smiled at Hal's obvious jab, and Hal winked playfully.

"Are you telling me that you are?" Sphinx asked her without much concern. "I have seen no proof of this, but it is not as though we meet socially. Perhaps I am mistaken."

She had to scowl at that. "No, you're right. Not that my relations would know that, as we are not close, but all the same, I am no fashion plate."

Tilda huffed loudly. "You're a bloody rotten pair, the both of you. Ungrateful wretches."

"Tilda…" Hal pleaded, fearing they might have actually offended the woman to such a degree as to earn her wrath.

"Hush," she said at once. "Did you think I did not notice that neither of you has any sense of fashion? I can assure you, I knew it from the first sight of you. As much as I would enjoy sending you off to make a spectacle of yourselves, I will resist the urge." She sniffed as though it was a grand and generous sacrifice on her part.

Belatedly, Hal thought of thanking her anyway out of sheer deference.

Luckily, her husband was much quicker. "We are very grateful," he said, and Hal could only hope he conveyed the proper sincerity in his expression.

If his face could contort in such a human way.

She was not entirely certain it could.

"You will be perfectly middling in the fashion you wear upon your arrival at your new destination," Tilda assured them as she began to form the shape of a waistcoat on Sphinx with rather bold fabric. "Enough that Hal's fashionable relatives will wrinkle their noses up and insist that you have a new trousseau ordered. Upon which suggestion, you will reply that, owing to your recent nuptials, you have a new trousseau that has been sent ahead of you to the finest modiste in Paris. I will provide you with the name and address, at which time, these sumptuous items will be made available to you."

Hal peered over the screen once more at the woman, looking impressed at the forethought.

"I see," Sphinx murmured, wincing as he craned his neck, no doubt against the flourishes of linen around his neck. "And then we will be the spectacle we need to be?"

Tilda hummed a laugh to herself. "Everyone is a spectacle in Paris, love. Which means that, in effect, no one is."

"Why don't I find that encouraging?" Sphinx asked aloud, looking over at Hal and meeting her eyes with longsuffering, cynicism, and, she was surprised to find, an odd light of humor.

She could have smiled, but she matched his longsuffering with a sigh instead. "Nor do I."

It was destined to be a short trip across the Channel, but as there were so few people aboard, it seemed as though it was taking ages and ages. Or perhaps that was only because his wife wasn't speaking to him.

She wasn't ignoring him, per se. At least, he didn't think so.

They hadn't even been married for twenty-four hours, and hadn't even managed a disagreement yet, let alone a fight. That was a minor miracle, considering their previous exchanges with each other. But then, the details of their mission had given them a lot to consider, and it was entirely possible that Hal was nervous.

This was her first assignment in the field, as he understood things, and without the full information, there wasn't much room for anticipation. Weaver had hosted the newlyweds the night before, after they had finished their costuming session with Tilda, and this morning he had driven them to the docks in his coach, giving them the information about where and when the next batch of information would come to them.

It was made perfectly plain to them, however, that none of that information was to be investigated during their Channel crossing.

Why, John hadn't felt the need to ask, but he could only presume that Rogue, Trace, or his brother Jeremy, known as Rook, had some suspicions about the situation, if not direct information.

It wasn't exactly likely that the information came from Trace, as he had only been reinstated a few weeks ago, but the other two…

Not that it mattered. Shortly before they left port, a sailor pushed past John roughly, grunting a sort of apology as he did so, leaving a parcel beneath John's arm when he readjusted his path off the ship.

Without a word, John had handed the parcel to Hal with a warm smile. She'd returned it with a dazzling version of her own, and wordlessly slipped the parcel into the drawing portfolio at her side.

It sat in there now, folded between sketches and notes and what not as though it was only a parcel of extra sheets for her drawing.

Their first action as a team, and they had succeeded without a word.

Surely, that was significant.

But there was no time for victory or exhilaration over it, as much as he was relieved by her immediately understanding of what he needed her to do. They were in character at all times in public, at attention whenever they could be observed, and there could be no discussion of anything in any way sensitive when they could be overheard.

They hadn't exactly discussed their characters, though. There hadn't been time, and the evening before had been one of hastily delivered instruction and advice. He'd been up half of the night going over what he had been told and running through coded puzzles he used to train himself before any significant project began. His mind needed to be quick, quicker than it had ever been, and his eyes needed to see everything he could possibly see.

His wife had been sleeping in the next bedchamber over.

It had never once occurred to him that their wedding night ought to have been spent together. Until this moment, it hadn't occurred to him that the night before had actually *been* his wedding night. The marriage was a legal arrangement, nothing more.

And yet, all they had in this mission of theirs was each other. From all accounts, they would have little by way of allies in France, apart from what lay in the information contained in Hal's portfolio. The only person he could be absolutely certain of in this whole affair was Hal.

His wife.

Surely, they could set aside old grievances, pitiful though they were.

She was outspoken, and every professional situation they'd met in had displayed that. He'd never reacted well to that, preferring to commence with the business at hand, and they'd had a few minor spats about it. Thankfully, they rarely worked together directly, even if they were both involved in the same mission. Now, they were literally side by side, and their combating natures had to be amended.

He, for one, would take a woman who could annoy him and grate his every nerve with exactness and put his life in her hands, and he would take her life in his own hands, though she likely thought him dull, arrogant, and proud.

Personal opinions could no longer matter where they were concerned.

Only the mission.

If she would not come to him and start them off, then he would take the first step.

Craning his neck against the impossibly tight, yet thankfully simple cravat at this throat, John moved across the deck of the ship towards Hal. She sat, strangely enough, on a large coil of rope as though it were an ottoman in any given drawing room in London. Her bonnet, once perfectly perched and tied atop her head, sat on the planks beneath her, the ribbons draped over her half-boots, her fair hair bared to the sunlight and glinting with it. A few curls danced free from the simple yet fashionable chignon she wore, and added much to the picture she presented, sprigged muslin, blue pelisse, and all.

His fair wife.

He wouldn't have called her fair yesterday; there was no denying, however, that fair she was.

She was busily, determinedly, sketching away.

John nodded at a passing crew member, and continued in Hal's direction, lifting his chin. "Sketching away, my dear? What, pray tell, has captivated your attention?"

A very slight smile crossed her lips, but she did not look up. "Why, you, husband."

"Me?" He did his best not to rear back and came to her side instead. "Why me?"

Hal glanced up, one brow arching. "Why not? I am fascinated by mysteries, and you are more a mystery to me than anyone."

"True enough, I suppose," he murmured. "May I see your progress?"

She shrugged and turned the paper towards him. "If you like. I've only made a start."

She had done a great deal more than that. John could not believe what he was seeing. Yes, the drawing was not complete, nor close to it, but its incompleteness only made the likeness all the more startling. She had captured his scowl, his jaw, the set of his shoulders, even the spacing of his eyes. He could have been looking at himself in the mirror, and no portrait his mother had commissioned had ever resembled him so accurately.

And she was not finished with it.

He'd heard rumors of the skills and abilities of Hal, but some corner of his mind had always dismissed them as elaborations.

This was proof of his folly, and it was uncanny.

"Good heavens, Hal." He shook his head, eyes wide. "I had no idea... That is incredible."

Color raced into Hal's cheeks, and she returned to the sketch, focusing on the hair above his left ear. "Thank you."

"When did you know you could draw an individual so accurately?" he asked, leaning against the railing behind him. "That is a gift."

Hal chuckled, the sound lower than John expected to hear. "When I was ten, the portrait I made of my father was less than flattering. He claimed I had to do it again for better practice, and I assured him that was what he looked like." She paused in her sketch and looked up at John again. "My mother took one look at my drawing and said, 'Oh, zat is quite right. *Très bien, ma chérie.*'" She quirked her brows. "The pair of them had quite a row over it. I believe he was consoled enough in the end."

John smirked rather wryly. "No doubt."

Her cheeks colored again, and John realized belatedly how it could have been taken, and what it would imply about Hal's parents.

Hardly a promising beginning for the pair of them as a couple.

"Say what you will about my parents," Hal said quietly, her pencil flying across the page as she continued her sketch of him, "they were devoted to each other."

John frowned at hearing that. "I know nothing of your parents, Hal."

She continued to draw. "You never read the reports?"

"What reports?"

Her pencil paused, and she blinked, though she did not look up at him. "I thought everyone in the Offices knew my circumstances."

"Then I must not be everyone," he quipped, surprised that he could do so with lightness. He was usually too dry for such things, too serious for joviality, and too unsociable for easy conversation.

Yet here he was.

"It's not a conversation for here." Hal shook her head and straightened, cocking her head as she examined her drawing for a moment. "When the time is more appropriate, I'll tell you about them."

He nodded in full comprehension, though her words were innocent enough. He'd suspected that her family had ties to the covert operations in which they found themselves currently embroiled, and their present situation did not allow for the sort of sensitive information their story could contain.

"If you feel I should know," he told her with a shrug of one shoulder. "I'll not pry."

"It's not particularly personal," she laughed. "Confidential, perhaps, but I have no qualms in sharing it. Particularly considering what we're about to venture into, there are likely relevant details there."

John exhaled, looking out across the Channel. "Interesting. Speaking of relevant details, care to share any information about the relations with which we will be staying?"

Again, Hal laughed, and this time she put aside her drawing completely to turn towards him. Clasping her hands around her knees, she settled more fully onto the rope coil. "The family name is de Rouvroy, and I've only just learned that he is a baron. *Le baron* is my mother's first cousin. The title is not their legacy, but what was bestowed by Napoleon for services rendered. The family title was stripped in the Revolution, but they all kept their heads, so to speak."

"How did they manage that?" John asked, bemused by the tone of entertainment his wife had taken on.

"Their loyalties lie with whoever is in power. You'll find their living beyond what you would expect of a humble baron, and that is quite simply because of their convenient alliances. The house is the family estate going back hundreds of years. They move in particularly high circles, so as much as we hated it, going to Tilda was likely crucial to our success." She made a face of disgust and shuddered.

John found himself chuckling at that. "I shall endeavor to see it as such, though I suspect it will have a bitter taste for quite some time."

Hal nodded eagerly in agreement. "I fear we will be trotted out to court, and we must look like the sort of relations the baron would have."

"Well," he sighed in response, "investigating high circles is likely our best starting place as it is. Your cousin will probably have excellent connections for us to explore."

"In all circles, I am sure," Hal remarked dryly. She indicated several different levels with her hand, widening her eyes.

"All the better. I think we will have a need to see to those." He folded his arms and glanced down at her. "How should we play this, Hal? And should I call you something other than Hal? Before your family, at least."

Hal paused in her almost giddy attitude and position, her eyes widening, and she straightened up. "I hadn't considered… My mother always called me *Ange*, given she couldn't manage my name well. It's not very French, after all."

John gave her a half-smile. "Would you like me to call you *Ange*? Or the English version?"

Hal's shy smile did something to his stomach, flipping it over in a strange way. "*Ange* would be fitting. If you don't mind."

"Not in the least," he managed, his stomach still feeling like a beached fish flopping awkwardly. "And you may call me John, unless you really want the formality of Pratt."

"You want your name out there?"

"If yours is out there, mine might as well be, too." His half smile spread to a full one easily. "Believe me, no one in Paris knows who I am."

Hal chuckled and nodded with warmth. "I can believe that. I think travelling outside of England too extensively would create a rash of some sort upon your skin."

John frowned playfully, though there was certainly some truth to the jest. "I will have you know that I have been to the Continent several times, and only received a slight chill coming out of Spain."

Hal's jaw dropped before she erupted into peals of laughter, tossing her head back, her throat dancing with each laugh, her eyes squeezed shut.

Beautiful.

There was no other word for it. No separating the sight from the sound, nor either from the feeling it invoked. It was quite simply beautiful, and there was no denying it. The truth of it squeezed his chest as if in a fist with fingers digging in.

Painful sensation, but a pleasant experience.

Now *that* was a puzzle.

"I thought your brother was the amusing one," Hal managed as her laughter began to subside. "Who'd have thought you knew humor at all?"

"Harsh," he protested. "Who do you think taught my brother the humor he is known for?"

Hal gave him a dubious look, echoes of laughter still in her features. "Not you, Pratt, and that is the truth."

There was no reason for her to think otherwise, and he knew it well. He smiled and waved dismissively. "You think that if you like."

She rolled her eyes and sighed. "As for how we play this…" She shrugged, turning somber. "Disenchanted? The nature of it can vary based on what we need, but I don't know how else to go."

"I agree, actually."

Hal's eyes went round. "We agree? Good heavens, what happened?"

John met her eyes frankly, smiling slightly. "We got married."

She snorted once. "As if that's the solution to any problem. Surely, it only creates more of them."

"As this is my first one," he said without hesitation, "I'll reserve judgment upon the state until I've experienced it a bit longer. Kindly refrain from ruining the thing for me."

A sharp blow struck his shins and his legs jerked back, causing him to stumble slightly, though he laughed freely. "*Et tu, Ange?*"

"Don't mix your languages," his wife scolded as he straightened. "Now leave me be, Pratt. I've a drawing to finish, and I want to take in more of this glorious breeze while the other passengers take ill in their cabins."

John bowed politely, inclining his head. "It just so happens that I am well and whole, too, so I will stroll about the deck enjoying the quiet. Until later, wife."

"Until later, husband."

Chapter Four

"Hal, wake up. Hal."

The low, gentle voice dragged her from sleep, and the boot pressing on her knee and rustling her stirred her from the position she had taken for that sleep. She pushed to an upright position from the wall of the coach and rubbed at her eyes.

"How long have I been asleep?"

"Since we left Cormeilles," Pratt replied in a low grumble. "You were fortunate enough to drift off again almost immediately. I don't know how you managed that. I feel as though my head has been trampled under our horses' hooves from the time we left Beauvais last night."

Hal blinked hard, the tension in her head roaring back to life at his words. "You had to say something, didn't you?" She pinched the bridge of her nose hard, then paused and opened her eyes again, her hand flying back to her lap. "Did you say I've been asleep since Cormeilles?"

"I did," he grunted, managing to cross one leg over the other in the space of the coach without even brushing her skirts. "Why?"

She looked out of the window, blinking again at the passing scenery, and the light cascading down upon it. Her eyes widened and flicked back to her husband. "It has to be close to midday. Cormeilles is barely ten miles outside of Paris. How in the world has it taken so long to go so short a distance?"

Pratt gave her a very flat, very bland smile, looking as fatigued and haggard as any man alive ever had. "We have averaged roughly five miles an hour for the majority of our trip from Calais, Hal. Since Cormeilles, we have been slower than that, likely on account of the poor conditions of the road, which makes your ability to sleep during that time all the more astonishing."

"One of my lesser known gifts," she murmured in shock, sitting back against the seat of the coach and staring at him in bewilderment. "Less than five miles an hour? Are you sure?"

"Believe me, I have made a very careful study of our speed and course in the last thirty-six hours." He cocked his head, his eyes narrowing. "How did you know that Cormeilles was ten miles outside of Paris?"

One side of Hal's mouth quirked. "I looked at a map before we arrived in Calais."

Pratt raised a brow. "And you remembered Cormeilles specifically and the distance it was from Paris? Calais was nearly two days ago."

"One of my better-known gifts," Hal said simply as she allowed the rest of her mouth to complete the smile. "I have a rather exact memory. If I see something, I can remember it with a startling accuracy. If I focus on something with some effort, I'm likely to never forget it."

Now it was he whose eyes widened, and he seemed to still completely in the uncomfortably jolting coach. "What I wouldn't give for that ability."

Hal laughed once. "It is not always agreeable, but in your case, yes, I can see how that would be useful." She glanced out of the window again. "I take it we have entered Paris."

"*Oui*," Pratt replied with a heavy sigh, "and I have never been so pleased to see any place in my life. I may embrace *le baron* simply for being at the end of the journey."

"I wouldn't recommend it," Hal told him with a playful wince. "I am not at all assured of the nature of my mother's departure from her family all those years ago, so we may find ourselves coldly received."

Pratt stared at her in a resigned sort of study. "Now you mention this."

An earnest grimace exchanged places with the playful wince on her face. "I didn't want to worry you."

"What I feel now is worry," he assured her. "Had I known before, I could have replaced worry with strategy. Now…?"

"Now?" she prodded when he trailed off.

He groaned and rubbed at his brow. "Now I am too bloody tired for strategy, which leaves me with worry, which is not at all comforting, and I'm presently feeling it will be a miracle if we are not shot on sight."

"It won't be *that* bad," she told him with a laugh that she didn't feel.

Truth be told, it could be that bad. Her mother hadn't said much about her family in France over the years, though she had continued to correspond with some of them. Everything her mother had done had seemed contradictory, though her love for her husband and children had been constant. She had likely been as involved with covert operations as her husband, and given that she had left her family to marry Hal's father, seemingly without the approval of her family, one had to assume she had devoted herself to the British.

But there had always been rumors.

Not among polite society, of course. They had all declared Marguerite Mortimer the most beautiful creature to come out of France, though she had been criticized for bearing the aloof, haughty nature that had spurred on the bloody revolution in her home country.

In the darker, more secret circles that Hal and her brother occupied, however, the lines were rather blurred.

"Where did you stash our private correspondence?" Pratt asked in a low voice as they turned down another row of pristine houses. "As we weren't detained entering Calais, I must presume that the examiners found nothing?"

Hal shuddered at the memory of being so humiliated as to be examined nearly to the square inch of her by females designated by the customs officials at the port. It was all in an effort to prevent the smuggling in of goods and no doubt various items of a more nefarious nature, but it was shockingly thorough. One could only presume that their belongings had undergone an equally thorough looking over.

"Yes," she managed, returning her attention to Pratt. "Not on my person, and not in my trunk."

"And you managed that how?" he inquired with mild interest, either for his own benefit or for the sake of maintaining a steady stream of conversation to ease the cordiality he would shortly need.

She wasn't quite sure how out of practice a man like Sphinx would be.

Pratt, she reminded herself with a mental kick. *Pratt.*

She had to think of him as such for the duration of the mission, or their objective would be completely compromised.

"There is a false bottom in my trunk," Hal informed him with a quick smile. "My father had it installed when I was eleven or so. Told me it would be a marvelous place to keep my secrets when we travelled as a family. I rather think now that he might have kept *his* secrets in there, but it did well enough." She shrugged and glanced out of the window at the passing buildings and inhabitants of Paris walking about.

Strange how a place could look so like another in some ways, and yet so very strange in others. They might have been on a neighborhood street in Mayfair for the appearance of their surroundings, only there was a sort of haunted feel to the streets of Paris. As though the buildings themselves could tell the tales the city had seen in the last fifty years.

If not longer.

"Are you nervous?" Pratt asked in a low voice she couldn't interpret well.

Hal shook her head but swallowed so hard it surely betrayed her. "I've never been particularly good at pretense."

"Nor I," he confessed.

She laughed once without an ounce of humor in it. "Then what the devil are we doing here?"

Pratt exhaled without smiling, though there seemed to be amusement in the sound. "I'm sure we'll find out by and by. So for now, let's just be delighted to be out of the damned carriage and to see your family."

"Family is an interesting choice of word," she murmured as the carriage pulled to a stop before a house identical to the one beside it. "Relations are all I can claim of them."

"Well, let us hope they see you as more than that," Pratt grunted as he leaned forward to grab the handle of the door, only to find a prompt footman already opening it. "If they don't, we will have a rather awkward time of it in Paris for the duration of our stay." He quirked his brows knowingly, his expression almost derisive.

Hal made a face back, though Pratt had already disembarked and missed it. "Yes, thank you, husband," she muttered. "So encouraging. Really."

His hand was extended, as it was her turn to climb out, and she took it, remembering, belatedly, that she had removed her gloves at some point in the coach. The touch of his skin against hers was almost jarring in its intensity, though it was a simple matter of palm to palm, fingers around fingers. He was warmer than she expected, and the heat of him raced into her arm, drawing her closer to him as she stepped to the ground.

Not gracefully, given that she nearly swayed into him with that final step, which, when combined with the odd squawk that came from her mouth, gave the impression that she had stumbled worse than the reality.

Pratt gripped her other arm with a quick snatch. "Steady. Are you all right?"

An embarrassed heat raced into her cheeks, and she shook her arm free while her hand still held his. "Fine," she snapped, fidgeting with her traveling gown in an attempt to recover some dignity. "The step was not sturdy."

"Of course."

There was no irony in his tone, and for some reason, that was worse.

"Thirty-six hours in a coach with you has left me in a vile temper," Hal grumbled, glaring up at him. "Don't provoke me before I'm forced to be pleasant for show."

"In what way have I provoked you?" Pratt inquired in the same dry, mild tone he'd used all morning as he led her to the door of the house. "All I said was…"

"Not another word," she ground out, gripping his hand. "I beg you."

Incredibly, he listened and complied, giving her hand a gentle squeeze in return.

Hal exhaled slowly, the pressure in that squeeze grounding her as her anticipation rose. As in all else in this mission, she was playing a part, acting to accomplish the task at hand, scheming for opportunities to unearth what she could. But this moment before her would bear more truth than anything else she would endure for some time.

This was the home of her legitimate family, actual relations that would be hosting them, and she was about to properly make their acquaintance for the first time in her life.

Anticipation and anxiety ran a footrace within her at the prospect. Swallowing was impossible, breathing unbearable. And she was exhausted.

The door of the house opened as they approached, a second footman stepping out and moving to join the first to help with their trunks. Then an older gentleman with greying temples stepped out and snapped a bow.

"*Madame Pratt, Monsieur Pratt.* Welcome. *Le baron* and ze family will please greet you inside."

"Thank you," Pratt replied in a clear tone, sliding his hand from Hal's to offer a more polite arm to her, which she took in the same smooth motion.

At least the butler would find them collected and proper, even if no one else would.

Hal continued silently beside Pratt as they moved into the house, following the butler within, her throat going dry and tightening all at once.

What if her mother had grossly offended her French relations before she left, and this was all just a dramatic plot that would end with her being thrown out onto the streets of Paris with her sham of a husband? She had no other connections in France, and she doubted Pratt did, either. Everything in the mission hinged on them being able to move about in high circles, and without any other operatives to confer with safely, changing the tone of said mission would be infinitely more difficult.

There hadn't been time to wait for an answer to the letter she'd sent to her mother's cousin, practically inviting herself and her new husband to stay with them, so she had no assurance that they wanted the company.

But they had been let in, almost as though they had been expected.

Would they now be informed that there was no room for them here? Or that their would-be hosts would rather not be hosts?

Hal found herself looking around the entry as they stood in it, and her breath caught at the finery she saw. Gilded edges to nearly every surface from ceiling to floor, exquisite artwork adorning that ceiling, and the marble beneath their feet glistened, echoing every step placed upon it. Even the sconces on the walls were gilded, and the candles within them burned brightly despite it being the middle of the day with plenty of daylight streaking through the windows.

There was no sense to that but to reveal a complete lack of concern for the cost of candles, nor the wasting of them.

Strange.

"Zis way, monsieur, madame." The butler gestured down a corridor somehow even more gilded than the entrance hall, and it was only then that Hal realized she had been gawking like an urchin in a palace.

Apparently, her husband had as well.

"I feel as though I will dirty something just by being in the same room," Hal muttered out of the corner of her mouth. "Why is everything white and gold?"

Pratt said nothing beside her and only continued moving in the direction the butler led them, attention fixed ahead.

Hal frowned up at him. "Say something."

One edge of his mouth lifted just enough to give her an indication of life. "You told me not to provoke you. I'm doing my best to accommodate that instruction."

A startled chuckle erupted from her, and she clamped her free hand over her mouth, the brief sound of her laugh echoing off the pristine surfaces of the house. Hal squeezed her eyes shut and found herself curving into Pratt's side in an attempt to recover herself as more giggles bubbled up.

"But if you would like my insight," Pratt went on, seemingly unruffled by her current state of hilarity, "I will admit that I find the expanse of white to be slightly unnerving when not dressed in finery. The gold is an elegant touch, but I have the strangest sense of being in a palace rather than a residence."

"It would seem that the family fortunes are intact, even if the title is not," Hal murmured between snickers, straightening herself up and facing forward yet again. "Perhaps Tilda's efforts were not in vain."

Pratt grunted once. "After seeing the adornments in this house, I will kiss Tilda's feet when we return to England, mark my words."

Hal grinned up at him, her nerves miraculously abated for the time being. "Consider them marked."

He smiled at her in return, and the strangest sense of unity filled her, despite the ache in her head, the fatigue in her limbs, and the general sense of being covered in dust from their travels. Even if the worst happened and they were tossed out, at least she would have him by her side.

Whether or not that was worth anything remained to be seen, but there was some solace in not facing this alone.

"Are you ready, *Ange*?" Pratt asked in a quiet voice, the blend of green and brown in his eyes seeming to swirl with a hidden depth to the question.

Or perhaps that was the endearment.

"More ready now than a moment ago," Hal admitted as she allowed her arm to curl more fully into his. "Thank you."

One of his brows lifted. "For…?"

Hal rolled her eyes. "I've never known you to be more amusing or agreeable than you have been in the last few days, and I can only imagine you are doing so in an effort to set me at ease. Or to rid me of my doubts. Whatever your reasons, I am appreciative."

"I haven't the faintest idea what you are talking about. Perhaps your initial perceptions were incorrect, and now you are seeing the truth of me."

"Perhaps…" She drew the word out, hesitation palpable. Then she pursed her lips. "And perhaps I am truly an opera dancer who trained in Italy and this entire excursion is only an opportunity to perform in Paris."

Pratt only exhaled with more noise than he usually did. "I knew it."

Hal bit her lip hard, fearing she might actually draw blood as she forcibly restrained laughter. A hum resembling a weak laugh escaped, but the rest remained within her chest, bouncing off her ribs and lungs until she feared she'd strain for her next breath.

The butler suddenly turned to his left and bowed. "*Monsieur, madame, vos invités sont arrivés.*"

"Help," Hal squeaked, laughter still warring within her.

"Inhale…" Pratt instructed with a small smile, waiting for her to do so. "Exhale…"

She obeyed again, slowly, then nodded as the laughter faded, leaving only exhaustion behind.

Which had been there before her laughter, so she supposed all was well.

Nodding once more, Hal lifted her chin and turned to face the doorway to the next room, proceeding forward when the butler stepped back. Her fingers brushed absently against Pratt's sleeve, and his free hand covered hers in an almost automatic response.

There was something quite sweet about that.

She turned her attention to the overdressed parlor they were entering, and the people within.

A taller gentleman with greying hair and a fairly trim, though admittedly sluggish, frame smiled with what appeared to be genuine warmth. He wore no jacket, only shirtsleeves and a vest, his cravat middling in flourishes, and there was something about the way his dark eyes crinkled that Hal instantly liked.

"*Mon petit Ange*," he said in a newly booming voice. "*Bienvenue, bienvenue*!"

Hal smiled with more sincerity than she had intended, the impulse an involuntary one in the face of his good humor. "*Monsieur le baron*," she greeted, curtseying with more perfection than she had ever managed in her entire life.

"*Non*," he urged, coming to her quickly and taking both hands. "*Non, ma petite*, we shall not stand on ceremony here. No titles. Please, call me Jean, or de Rouvroy, if the formality pleases you." He kissed both hands, then leaned in to kiss both cheeks.

"*Merci*," Hal murmured, blushing just a little. She turned to indicate Pratt beside her. "This is my husband, Mr. Pratt."

De Rouvroy looked at Pratt with an equally warm smile. "Monsieur, you are most welcome, to my home and to my family."

Pratt bowed in return. "*Merci beaucoup, monsieur.*"

De Rouvroy nodded politely and turned back to Hal with a sigh. "*Ma douce cousine.* So much like your *maman.* Not the eyes, though. Dark eyes, she had."

Hal returned his nod, still smiling. "She did, and I do not resemble her so much. I take after my father."

"Ah, but the same *esprit* is there." He grinned and tapped her cheek gently. "*Juste là.*" He exhaled with some unspoken emotion, then turned, brightening. "Allow me to introduce you to *ma famille*."

A surprisingly young woman stood by an ornate divan, her gown too elegant for a day at home with family but flattering in the extreme. Where de Rouvroy was aging, albeit well, this woman could have sprung from the fountain of youth itself. She could not have been more than a year or two older than Hal, unless her eyes were deceiving her. Her dark, sable hair was pulled back with fashionable simplicity, emerald ear bobs dangling along the ringlets surrounding them, and while her smile did not bear the same warmth as her husband's, it was rather pleasant in its own right.

"*Cousine*, Mr. Pratt," de Rouvroy intoned with a heartfelt formality, "*ma femme* Victoire, Madame de Rouvroy."

Victoire curtseyed effortlessly, her hands cradling a swelling in her belly Hal hadn't noticed initially. "Welcome," she greeted softly almost without accent. She gestured to nearby seats. "Please, join us. I will send for some tea."

"*Madame*," Hal protested, shaking her head. "My husband and I have been traveling without stopping since Calais. We are rather dusty, I fear, and your furniture…"

"*J'insiste*," Victoire overrode without hesitation, her smile spreading. "The chairs were made for sitting, *non*? You are not so filthy as to ruin them. You must be exhausted, do sit."

De Rouvroy chuckled and gestured to the chairs as well. "You should do as she says," he encouraged. "She is quite fierce in her opinions."

Hal managed a smile and nodded once. "Fair warning, cousin. I am likely to drift off if I sit for too long in a comfortable place."

"And I would shortly follow," Pratt admitted without any of the stiffness she'd expected of him.

"We shall not keep you long," de Rouvroy told them both. "A bit of nourishment and then off to your rooms for rest and *récupération*, *oui*?"

Hal sighed as she moved to her chair, her smile spreading. "*Oui. S'il vous plaît.*"

Victoire laughed as they all sat. "Ze journey from Calais can be very trying if you have no place to rest along the way. Ze roads alone are *très misérable*."

"They are indeed," Pratt agreed, crossing one knee over the other beside Hal. "*Ange* here managed to sleep despite them, but I could not."

"Impressive, *cousine*," de Rouvroy praised warmly. "I cannot manage so myself. That road is not so good as the English roads, I think."

Hal tilted her head as tea was brought in. "Have you been to England?"

"*Oui*," came the simple reply. "Several times. Ze roads are better there, but our opera is better here." He winked with a chuckle as he indicated that they should help themselves to the tea.

"I do hope to see it," Hal said before she could help herself, stirring a bit too much sugar into her tea.

Her cousin's eyes lit up. "Ah! We attend the opera regularly, *ma petite*, and you shall attend with us! There are marvelous operas in Paris at present, are there not, Victoire? Indeed, we shall attend them all, I daresay."

Pratt cleared his throat very softly as Hal added yet another cube of sugar to her tea just to busy herself. She paused, cursed silently, and sat back, cautiously lifting her tea and saucer with her as she stirred the overly sugared mess before her.

She enjoyed the opera, but hardly in excess. She'd hoped to attend once, perhaps twice, as the Paris Opera was rumored to be the best in Europe. But if their whole interaction with the higher society of Paris was relegated to only the opera and nowhere else…

She hissed to herself in a sort of scolding, wondering just what her husband would make of that.

His hand slid to her arm, gently patting as he leaned forward to situate himself with tea.

Well, there was that, at least.

If he were truly bothered, surely he would have gripped her arm rather than pat it.

"I confess," Pratt ground out, reaching for a small piece of cake alongside the tea set, "I am not one for lofty music, but I can appreciate a well-performed aria as well as any with a working set of ears. Within reason, of course, and provided I am not inundated with an excessive quantity."

Perhaps not.

Luckily for them both, de Rouvroy chuckled. "Never fear, Pratt, I shall devise various opportunities to introduce my beautiful *petite cousine* to all of Paris. But you shall love the opera before you leave our fair city, I stake my word on that." He grinned with an almost mischievous air, then turned to his wife. "René would be an excellent tutor for them in the opera, would he not, *mon chérie*?"

Victoire nodded with almost as much eagerness as her husband expressed. "*Oui!* He is always wishing for more of the opera, and he has such elegant friends!" She looked at Hal with bright eyes. "My husband's son from his first wife, you know. Such a well-behaved young man, and so good to his siblings, even the young ones."

"He has enough of them to be sure," de Rouvroy laughed without shame. "Alas for him and my sweet Agathe, there were only they two for so long, but now…"

On cue, several small voices cried out in delight from somewhere else in the house, drawing fond smiles from their parents. This was followed by a crash of some sort, followed by loud laughter and the thundering of many small feet.

Hal exhaled slowly and turned to look at her husband, wide-eyed and contrite.

He silently met her eyes, his own unreadable, and quietly sipped his tea.

Chapter Five

There was much to be said for the benefits and positive influence of a night of excellent rest and quiet solitude upon a body riddled with fatigue and exhaustion. John couldn't recall what they were, having not had such in some time, but he did hope that this evening would allow him to reacquaint himself with the sensation, if not its privileges.

At the moment, however, he was allowing a sallow-faced servant to act as his valet. No doubt he was desperate to prove himself to *le baron* so that he might one day have the hope of serving him as valet rather than attending on the few guests who might come.

John could not imagine a family with as many children as the baron and his wife had actually entertaining on a particularly regular basis.

If only John could give the lad some work worth demonstrating to his master.

Unfortunately, he didn't care about cravats or waistcoats or any such thing, and until he and Hal ventured out to the modiste who had all of their finery, and no doubt much of their intelligence from the Shopkeepers, there would be very little of interest for Leys to do.

"Would monsieur like for me to fetch a pin for ze cravat? Pearl would well suit, or perhaps emerald?" Leys asked as he fussed again.

John shook his head once. "No thank you, Leys." He craned his head as he examined his appearance in the looking glass, grateful he didn't own anything so ridiculous as what the valet was suggesting.

He caught the disappointment in the lad's face, and a twinge of guilt flared in the pit of his stomach.

"After a long day of travel," John went on, as though he were continuing a thought rather than adding one, "I have no energy to attempt finery. The rest of our belongings shall be fetched tomorrow, I believe, and then I shall require much of your opinion, taste, and skills to ensure I do not embarrass myself or my wife among Paris society."

The brightening of his erstwhile valet's countenance did little to remove the guilt swirling in John's gut, and instead added unto it a sickening feeling of dread that was entirely selfish.

"*Oui, monsieur. Merci.*" Leys bowed too deeply for John's status and practically bounced out of the room.

Lovely. Now John would be turned into a peacock even if Tilda had managed some restraint in her selections.

Muttering under his breath, he moved to the side door of his bedchamber and pushed into the sitting room that connected his rooms to Hal's.

"Hal!" he called, not bothering to pretend at politeness here in their rooms. Not when he was this tired and this irritable. "Hal!"

"What?" she replied in a sharp tone from behind the door. "Gracious, Pratt, I'm barely presentable and about to rip my hair out, what do you want?"

He bit back a snarl and pounded his fist on the door.

"What?" she hollered back, her voice seeming to crack with irritation. "Come in, for pity's sake!"

Rolling his eyes, John pushed open the door and strode in, pausing a step only slightly when he caught sight of the woman within.

Hal had changed into a gown fit for a ballroom in London, the shade that of palest green, a string of pearls wound around her neck, and while he would doubt the ladies of London would have envied her gown, outdated though it surely was, he'd be damned if he'd find a fault in it. Her golden hair was braided, curled, and piled up in a style he'd never seen anywhere before, but it suited her, and it suited her well.

Very well.

"What?" Hal barked for the third time, drawing his attention to her face, where a scowl sat as prominently as her hair upon her.

He blinked and forced his expression into something fairly bland. "Let's get this over with. I haven't slept nearly long enough to be in a mood for company."

"And you think I am?" she shot back. "Look at this monstrosity." She jabbed a finger to indicate her hair. "Colette insisted that, since I want for a fine gown, my hair must compensate." She said the word with a distinctly French accent, deliberately mocking the maid who must have only recently left.

"I like it," John admitted with a shrug, eyeing it as one might a masterpiece of architecture.

"Then you wear it and see if it doesn't make your head ache." Hal huffed and turned her back. "Now, do me up. I was so vexed with Colette that I sent her out before I was ready for fear of lashing out at her."

John stared at the back before him, eyes widening at the open vee of skin below the slightly bowed neck.

Four buttons, perhaps five.

He had never done up a woman's buttons in his life, and here his wife…

His wife…

Dammit.

With a scowl of his own, John closed the distance between them, fingers extended towards the material with a single-mindedness he usually saved for his work. "Surely, it's not *that* bad."

Hal snorted softly, lowering her head a little, unwittingly bearing more of her neck to his view. "Remind me to have you pull the pins when we retire, husband. Then you may make assumptions on my hair."

John exhaled a wry laugh as he fastened her buttons, trying not to twitch every time his fingers brushed skin. Not that there was anything amiss with doing so, it was just…

Well, it was Hal's skin he was brushing against.

He didn't like her.

Did he?

"I see you've escaped with a moderately sensible cravat," his wife said with a far more pleasant tone. "How did you manage? Even I could see that Leys prefers a peacock."

"And I fear he will have one." John shook his head as he did up the last two buttons. "I may have told him we are fetching our better belongings, and then he may have more to do."

Hal nearly hit his head with her own as she tossed her head back to laugh heartily. "You didn't! Whatever possessed you to say something so absurd?"

"I haven't the faintest idea, but I regretted it the moment the words escaped." He nodded to himself with some pride as he finished the buttons, then patted a hand safely on Hal's shoulder to signal his task was complete. "There. Done up and ready."

She grunted softly, turning to face him with a dubious look. "That will depend on what one considers as ready. For the present, I call it awake and dressed."

"Strangely, I quite agree." He offered his arm to her without any gusto. "Shall we?"

She looped her arm through his and heaved a sigh. "I'll give you ten pounds if you can find a way to get us out of supper early without scandalizing or offending anyone."

John smirked but found himself growing more weary at the thought of an entire meal with the exuberant family of the Baron de Rouvroy.

"I extend the same wager to you," he told his wife as he moved them to the door of her rooms. "Get us out of there, and I'll pay you."

"Deal, Sphinx."

"Deal, Sketch."

They exchanged tired, resolute smiles, then moved out into the ornate corridor in the direction John could only hope was that of the dining room. At the moment, he wasn't sure which way was right and which left.

Blessedly, they found the stairs that would lead them down, allowing John to breathe a silent sigh of relief. One obstacle gone, but so very many more to go, and in this state…

"How does a place look garish even in the evening?" Hal murmured to him as they entered the more public rooms of the house.

The words made him want to laugh, though he couldn't do so, and he glanced around to verify them. The same gold and white theme from before echoed the corridors here, the rugs beneath their feet exquisite in their design and expensive in their quality. Finery was everywhere, could not be avoided, would not be ignored. Every piece of art sat in frames that could have graced any palace in the world and fetched a fortune in any market on the streets. And the art itself would likely have done the same, if not better.

John half expected them to eat off plates entirely made of gold and with utensils encrusted with gemstones.

"I thought you said that their family title had been stripped," John said in a low voice, leaning close to her. "Wouldn't the fortune have also been returned to the Crown?"

Hal hummed a soft laugh. "One would imagine so, and yet *le baron* has not seemed to lose a single *centime* in all the troubles. It's extraordinary, don't you agree?"

John did agree, and he began to suspect…

He wasn't sure what he suspected, but the circumstances were all too fortunate in the baron's favor, considering what had happened within the rest of France. How could anyone succeed in such a way under both Napoleon *and* the monarchy? The coincidence was too convenient a thing for his taste. He wouldn't like to suspect Hal's relations, particularly given they were also hosting them.

Yet it could not be ignored.

It was far too early into their association with the baron and his family to have any real foundation for his suspicions, but he would not discount them, either. Something to keep his eye on, and that was all. But what else might he discover during his time here? Finery or no finery, if there was betrayal here, he would find it.

And that was an almighty if.

"If half of what I have heard about French cuisine is true, we could be in for a meal of extraordinary delights," he told Hal as they neared the dining room.

"If we have nothing but boiled potatoes and bread, I'll be delighted to eat more than I can stomach," Hal replied without a thought. "I don't care what it is, Pratt, because I will not be eating it in an inn or a coach."

"Amen to that." John forced a smile on his face. "Why does smiling hurt?"

Hal snorted once as she did the same. "Because you are so out of practice."

"Ah."

Entering the dining room, they found the family all there, including the children, and all seated before the guests had arrived.

Odd.

"*Mes cousins*!" de Rouvroy called as he caught sight of them, pushing to his feet with an eagerness that seemed uncalled for, considering the shortness of their acquaintance. "Please forgive us our informality. The children, you know, could not wait."

John could easily forgive the children; the question was why they were present at all.

"Of course," Hal murmured, her hand shifting almost awkwardly on John's arm.

"I see," de Rouvroy said with a small smile. "You disapprove of children at the table with adults?"

John shook his head at once. "No, not disapprove…"

"Surprise, then," the baron corrected. "For no doubt it is surprising to the genteel of the English to allow such noise during the evening meal."

Several rounds of giggles sounded from the table, and de Rouvroy turned to grin at them and put a shushing finger to his lips.

"Surprise would be a better description," Hal admitted, laughing herself. "I myself was not permitted a seat at the supper meal until I was twelve and could behave myself with decorum."

"And that, *ma petite*, is something which saddens me greatly." De Rouvroy gestured grandly to his family and stepped back to do so. "For what is the proper decorum of a child? Is it not to explore life and find joy in it? To give those of us who have lost some of our youth and exuberance a chance to revisit it? Why should we be so formal and expect them to ignore their natural inclinations when it will leave them all too soon?"

It was an extraordinary statement, especially for a member of the peerage, no matter which kingdom had bestowed it. No parent John had ever met in Society felt that way, even the best of them. Especially not while entertaining guests, though there was no telling how a family would behave in private.

John was a man of reserve and formality, one might say, though he could not admit to especially strong opinions on either subject. He simply saw no reason to alter what was accepted as proper behavior, nor to make any adjustments on his part in order to stand out. Indeed, all he had ever wanted from the times he was forced to attend in public circles was to blend in; to be as unobtrusive as possible.

Had he been that way by nature, or had the rules and traditions of English society made him so?

What a question to ask himself now. A simple family supper and he was questioning his own nature?

He must have been more fatigued than he thought.

"And we are not all assembled, you know," de Rouvroy continued when his guests had nothing to comment. "René and Agathe have not yet come down, but they will presently. May I introduce you to the young ones in the meantime?"

"O-of course," Hal stammered, still as locked in her position as he was.

"*Ici, mes enfants*," de Rouvroy instructed, gesturing up.

Five little ones popped to their feet, the youngest unable to be seen above the level of the table. Her siblings helped her to stand on a chair, and she grinned at now being so visible to the rest.

"First is Sophie," the baron informed them, the tallest girl with the darkest hair curtseying prettily at her introduction. "And beside her is Aimée. Our son is Paul, and then is Clara, and Marie."

The youngest did not so much curtsey as jump on the chair upon which she stood.

There was something to smile about in that.

De Rouvroy gestured again, this time for them to sit, and they did so without complaint or dramatics, though they did giggle as before.

"Oh, damn, did we miss the introductions?" drawled a decent imitation of an English accent from behind them.

John and Hal turned as one, parting briefly as they did so.

A dark-haired man with a startling likeness to the baron stood there with a pretty girl of perhaps sixteen, fair where her brother was dark, though the resemblance was unmistakable.

"Monsieur Pratt, Madame Pratt, may I present my son and my daughter? René, Agathe, this is Monsieur Pratt and our cousin Henrietta. Her *maman* was Marguerite, daughter of my uncle Claude." De Rouvroy looked at Hal with fond indulgence, even as the couples greeted each other with the deference politeness required.

"*Enchantée, cousine,*" René said with a smile not quite as warm as his father's, though certainly warmer than polite.

"*Merci,*" Hal murmured, looking a bit uncomfortable, which was not surprising after the day they'd had.

Mademoiselle de Rouvroy barely smiled at all as she looked at them, and only slipped her arm from her brother's and moved to the table, snapping off some command in French to her younger siblings, who did not seem the least bit perturbed at her tone.

Perhaps they were accustomed to an ill-tempered older sister.

Odd, though, for such a warm and congenial man to have a daughter as such. There was no accounting for personality, opinion, or willfulness, though. John's own brother was willful and impudent, while no one would ever accuse John of being so.

"You must forgive my sister, monsieur," René said as he stepped closer, his smile turning apologetic. "She does not take well to strangers, and I fear she is out of temper with our father at present."

"Not at all," John assured him as they moved to the table. "We are intruding upon your family home and are entirely at the mercy of your family's generosity and graciousness. Nothing to forgive, I can assure you."

René nodded in receipt of the statement. "*Merci, monsieur.* So good of you to say."

Then, nodding at Hal, he left them and moved to sit beside his youngest sister, whose name John had already forgotten, and was rather amiable with her given the discrepancy in their ages.

John moved to seat Hal just to the right of her cousin at the head of the table, assisting her with her chair, as any good husband would, then sitting, shockingly, beside her.

Husbands and wives rarely sat beside each other in polite company in England, but it was clear that these French relations of

Hal's considered this an informal family dinner, despite not truly knowing each other at all.

This would take some getting used to.

He forced a smile as he sat beside Hal and looked up the table at their host, who nodded, then bowed his head and offered a brief prayer in French, hardly giving John time enough to lower his head in deference before the thing was done.

Hal giggled very softly and turned it into a cough, reaching for her water as she glanced at John, the mirth still in her eyes.

If this was how their time here would be, he doubted either of them would come out of it unscathed. If they managed to get anything accomplished on their mission at all, it would be a miracle.

As they began to serve up the meal, chatter commenced around the table. Hal was very nearly interrogated as to her life in England, and anything that could be said about her mother seemed music to de Rouvroy's ears. Either he truly adored his cousin, or he was an actor of great skill, and John was struggling to tell the difference.

Yet another sign of his fatigue.

No one paid any particular attention to John, which he was quite grateful for. He had no desire to prattle on or to make his life seem in any respect more exciting or entertaining than it really was. He led a simple, scholarly life, apart from his ties to the covert operations in which he was now engaged, and it would be rather difficult to describe exactly what he did in a manner that would not bore the family to tears.

But from the sound of it, Hal's childhood had been particularly eventful. Her parents had traveled about the Continent from time to time and had brought their twins along with them on occasion. While she might not have attended suppers, by her own admission moments ago, she clearly benefited from her mother's peculiar parental tendencies, similar in style to her cousin, *le baron.*

"And how is your dear brother, then?" de Rouvroy inquired after slurping a spoonful of soup uncomfortably loudly. "I know your mother was not pleased about his being called Hunter, but your father would insist upon it."

Hal smiled at that, but John could feel the tension in it from where he sat. "Hunter is well enough. I don't know if you have heard, but he has left Society. Nearly ruined us all, you know, with his gambling and his ungentlemanly behavior. Quite a pariah now, and he seems content to remain so."

The baron looked sympathetic. "Oh, I am grieved to hear it. Is there nothing to be done to repair his reputation?"

"If he seemed at all repentant, it might help." Hal shrugged and dipped her spoon into the soup before her. "But alas, he is not, and will not be."

"Brothers can be a trial," Agathe broke in from her seat, glaring coldly at her own brother without any preamble.

René returned her look, wide-eyed and surprised. "*Qu'est ce que j'ai fait?*" he demanded.

Agathe gave no response and only shrugged as she buttered a roll from her plate.

"I have a brother myself," John broke in, unsure why he was doing so, turning his attention to the head of the table. "Younger. And he is a trial, as well, I can assure you."

Hal forced a laugh and nodded for effect. "Oh, that he is!" She smiled at de Rouvroy. "You'd like him, I think, cousin. Full of good humor and mischief, and practically irreverent about anything."

"It is a wonder, then, that you married this one," the baron remarked with a teasing lift of one brow.

John's stomach clenched, and it was all he could do to smoothly continue to eat his supper as if the statement meant nothing. As if he were completely secure in his wife's affections. As if the question had been asked dozens of times before.

As if the marriage had been one of choice.

"Oh, he wouldn't have done for me at all," Hal scoffed loudly, laughing at the very idea. "He is good for a laugh, I grant you, but in small dosages only. I would not trade my husband for his brother for anything. I have surely gained the better of the Pratt brothers, cousin, and I stand by my choice."

Choice.

But there hadn't been a choice. They could probably have done the mission without the marriage that had come with it, but the decision had not been theirs to make. She could have said no during the vows, he supposed, though it would have irritated their superiors that she was again making things difficult. She could have refused, and they would have made do.

She hadn't refused, but could she say she had chosen?

"That must give you some comfort, monsieur."

John blinked and looked up at the baron, unable to even pretend at a smile. "It does, sir. More than you know."

Hal's hand crept across the tabletop to cover his where it rested, then curved her fingers around his hand gently.

One heartbeat, perhaps two passed, and John shifted his own fingers enough to hold her hand as it held his.

Hal gave him a tiny smile, the pressure against his hand increasing for just a moment before she returned her attention to the baron. "Hunter did make an appearance at our very small wedding. Just long enough to do his duty and wish us well."

"Did you get a trousseau for your wedding?" Agathe asked with sudden interest. "You cannot go out in our society without the *parure nécessaire*. It would be an embarrassment."

"Never fear, *cousine*," Hal said with a smile that was more mischief than anything else. "We have all that we need, I promise you that."

Chapter Six

"Why does my hair feel even worse now than it did before?"

"Because *that* particular style is much worse than what you wore the other night."

Hal glared at her husband as he sat in the coach beside her. "That question did not require an answer."

"Then, you shouldn't have asked it aloud." Pratt shrugged and looked out of the window. "Why voice a question that doesn't require an answer? Waste of words."

"I have no qualms about hitting a man, Pratt. I have a brother who has borne my bruises," Hal told the infuriating man without looking at him. "Do not tempt me."

Pratt said nothing to this, which was to be expected, as he said nothing most of the time. He had said nothing all day, not that she had wanted him to. Left in the house of her cousin and his unending brood of children, Hal enjoyed nothing more than the silence her husband afforded her. The children were sweet and rather dear, but they were also wild, undisciplined, curious, and enthusiastic about anything and everything.

Hal was relieved she hadn't been brought up in such a way, even if her cousin thought it appropriate.

The only respite she'd had from the energy of the house was when they had gone to fetch their trousseau from Tilda's friend. The baron and his wife had been suitably impressed by the name they had given them, which settled both her and Pratt as to the nature of

Tilda's promises. If nothing else, they would be impressively arrayed, which ought to be enough to put them in the appropriate circles, if nothing else would.

There was one thing, however, that she had not settled on, in her mind or otherwise.

How the devil were they supposed to know who they were looking for? It would hardly be as obvious as a man or woman announcing themselves as a prescriber of Sieyès's beliefs, wishing for his dream to be fulfilled, recruiting others to join in a new order they were creating… All within earshot of the pair of them, of course.

It could not be so easy as that, but how would they know it? Where would they look? What would they have to suspect anyone of?

There were valid reasons that Hal had not been deemed a successful candidate for the covert world, and this was surely one of them.

How did anybody embarking on an assignment actually know where to start?

"I do believe I can hear you thinking, *Ange*." Pratt glanced at her as they rambled on in the coach. "What is the subject of such efforts?"

"Our mission." Hal lowered her voice, though they were alone in the carriage and no one could possibly hear her. "How in the blazes will we know what to look for? What if nothing is obvious? How do we even begin to…?"

"I was wondering the very same thing just now," he interrupted with a dry laugh. "With little to no information, apart from whatever is in your trunks and mine…"

She turned to him then, her pulse skipping. "We have to go through those tonight. It's likely we should have already done so."

Pratt snorted once. "When would we have had the time? Last evening, we barely made it through supper without falling asleep, and today, we were forced to endure entertainment before we fetched our costumes, then were foisted into ridiculous garb, scarfed down a quick supper, only to then be thrust into a coach so that we may suffer through an opera." He exhaled heavily, as though the mere recollection of the day's events was as exhausting as the day itself had been. "There was no time, *Ange.*"

"You don't have to call me that now," she reminded him, ignoring how her toes tingled every time he said it, particularly when his voice dipped lower on the final syllable. "We're alone."

Again, he shrugged. "Easier to remember to call you such in company if I call you such in private. I hope you don't mind."

"I don't," she quipped quickly. "Just reminding you." She looked down at the tips of her fingers, encased in pristine new gloves. "So tonight, we simply make acquaintances? I cannot see what else we can hope for without more information."

"Agreed. We'll use that inestimable mind of yours to remember faces and facts later. For now, we'll simply make ourselves known." He winced as the words escaped. "But not too much. A very subtle introduction to us."

Hal laughed and shook her head, much as the pinned monstrosity that was her hair protested the motion. "Well, I was hardly planning to announce us from the stage before the show began…"

"I wouldn't put it past you, if it served your ends." He gave her an all too knowing look, which was hardly fair, as he barely knew her.

She barely knew him, come to think of it. She realized she had been less than polite with him in the past, quick to take offense and snap back at presumed injuries. He was not a man of outward congeniality as his brother was; perhaps she had assumed the brothers shared a similar nature when, in fact, they were nearly opposite. Her judgements and assumptions had been ignorant where he was concerned, and she had little reason to think he'd done otherwise with her. But she had never doubted his abilities or his loyalties, and she'd never heard of him slandering her work either.

There was no such thing as a professional marriage, as far as Hal was aware, so she supposed that, mission-based or not, she might as well treat it as the connection it was.

"I'll have you know," she told him with a playful sniff, "that I happen to be remarkably reserved in company. Anything involving Society at all, and I barely speak a word."

The look of uncertain disbelief was worth the revelation, and she couldn't help but grin at it.

"That cannot be true."

She shrugged a shoulder. "It is. You would know if you saw me in company, but I never go out in it. My brother inherited all the charm and social affability my parents had to offer. I am always more content in intimate circles or on my own."

Pratt blinked, and Hal could almost feel his thought process, agile as it was, working on the idea. "Then we are destined to struggle in this mission of ours," he admitted slowly, "because I'm reserved no matter where I am."

"That is a slightly less shocking statement." She continued to grin, and he smiled in return.

He opened his mouth to reply when the coach stopped, bringing both of their attentions around to the building before them.

A line of carriages preceded them, and elegant people disembarked and made their way inside. Thankfully, many of the ladies had their hair coifed in a similarly ridiculous style as Hal.

If all else failed, at least she would not stand out because of her hair.

"Please don't be offended if I fall asleep during the performance," Pratt muttered as he moved to the door of the coach, which a gold liveried footman opened. He nodded and stepped out.

"I will ensure you do not," Hal returned as she followed, allowing him to help her down. "If I am to endure this, so must you."

He made a face, then extended an arm and looped her hand through it, sighing.

Cousin Jean, Victoire, René, and Agathe approached them, having ridden together in another coach, and the group moved into the theatre.

The general murmur of the public could have been described as a discordant hum that ebbed and flowed as though on a wave. Everywhere Hal looked, she saw finery and excess. While not the grandest theatre in Paris, and certainly nothing to the London Opera House itself, it was hard to think of anything lacking even in comparison. As with the de Rouvroy home, nearly every surface was gilded, shining with the luster of gold in the candlelight, and pristine in its artistry and workmanship.

The guests within, especially those currently lingering along with their group in the entrance and corridors of the theatre, could also fit that description.

Hal had never seen gowns of such detail and finery, and she had been to events in some of the highest circles in London. Not in some time, granted, but the memories of those events lingered in her mind with astonishing clarity. Nothing she had ever seen there compared with the excess before her now. Fortunes had clearly been spent on the gowns, and possibly hours on the ladies' hair alone, both of which seemed to be a waste to Hal. Some gowns clung to the fashions on their way into the catacombs of such wares while others were evidently the styles that were yet to come.

How could a matter of skirts, sleeves, and waistlines have so much influence on Society? What power did they wield, and how had they been granted it? And by whom?

Hal had never understood it, but she had to abide by the rules set down just as the rest of the ladies did. Reluctantly, as her unremarkable yet acceptable gown would testify, but abiding just the same.

She had never felt more out of place in her life, and that included any and all events in London.

"Remind me what we are seeing this evening, de Rouvroy," Pratt said in a surprisingly calm and seemingly interested tone.

The baron grinned as he led their procession down the crowded corridor. "In honor of you both, Pratt, we will enjoy *Elisabetta, regina d'Inghilterra.* Extraordinary music, simply marvelous."

Pratt only grunted and pasted a would-be pleasant smile on his face.

Hal pitied that false smile, least of all because it looked as though it pained him.

"I saw this when it played in London," Hal whispered to Pratt as they continued towards the box her cousin had reserved. "Middling at best. Rossini wrote the role of Elizabeth for his mistress."

"You aren't serious," her husband muttered back.

"I never jest about opera." She grinned up at him, nudging his side a little. "Don't worry, I heard that he married the woman a few years ago."

Pratt glanced at her, his lips curving just enough to be

encouraging. "Because that was my primary concern."

Hal snickered, covering her mouth to stifle the sound from her relations. Sometimes, her husband's dry humor really was quite perfect. Had she noticed that during their previous encounters? Not that she would have found anything praiseworthy in him, given their disputes and opinions in the past, but surely he'd shown some humor then.

Or had they only met under stressful situations where any sort of joviality, dry or not, would have been inappropriate?

If she knew anything about John Pratt, it was that he was never anything less than appropriate.

Never.

As they moved up the stairs, de Rouvroy began to wave at other guests and greet them warmly, his French taking on a more formal tone, though nothing in his behavior changed from the manner Hal had seen from him so far. All warmth and friendliness, all affability, and he seemed to know every single person who greeted him.

Hal marveled at her cousin and shook her head to herself. She had never been that person, and she would never be. Where he seemed to revel in the attention, she would have shrunk back from it. She knew a great number of people in Society, and they knew her, but she would flee from any occasion that would have involved being in the center of them.

Her cousin would have apparently preferred to collect them all and let the attention fall in showers of praise around him. This meant that whatever number of people were greeting her cousin, their attention would also fall upon her by association.

Her cheeks flamed in response to the realization, and she found herself tucking closer to her husband, though there was no shield anywhere from the curious eyes. The staircase was open to the level above, and so well attended was the opera this evening that those eyes were everywhere. Every aspect of Hal, of Pratt, of de Rouvroy, of them all, would be witnessed by anyone watching them. All scrutinized, all commented on, and all creating an impression, for good or for ill.

There was no comfort to be found in that.

None at all.

Don't trip. Don't slip. Don't fall.

She repeated the orders in her mind as she placed one foot in front of the other on the stairs, praying she did so with a modicum of grace. Poise had never really been an emphasis for her, more due to the lack of concern rather than a lack of necessity, yet now she felt that thread running through her spine and tugging herself upright. Could feel the books piled atop her head. Could feel the fingers beneath her chin pressing it up just enough to be perfect.

She could hear Miss Walker's instructions now and could feel the disappointment in her efforts.

That wasn't exactly the sort of feeling she wanted at the moment.

Perhaps now she could rewrite the past, in a way.

"Smile," Pratt murmured beside her. "We're not porcelain, even if we look it."

"This coming from you?" she murmured through her teeth. She managed a laugh. "You never smile."

"I'm a gentleman," he retorted. "Smiling is not required. Unfortunately, the same cannot be said for young ladies."

Hal would have snarled if her face had let her. "I'm not young."

"*Ange*," Pratt grunted. "Smile."

Something about the mixture of frustration and amusement in his voice made her *want* to smile, but the sound of his name for her was the only thing that actually brought a smile to her face. Not a grand one, that was beyond her during the best of times, let alone at a time like this, but a smile it was.

And somehow, doing so made her nerves ease just enough that she could breathe.

Rounding the top of the stairs, her hand still tucked neatly in Pratt's arm, Hal managed that small smile as well as glancing about, as though the attention her cousin encouraged was also welcomed by her.

Then her breath caught in her chest, and the smile froze on her lips.

Memory sprang to life, and the pages of its book spun as though by a breeze.

Who? Where?

"John," Hal whispered, barely managing the breath, her eyes

staring straight ahead now, her fingers digging into his arm.

"What?" he replied at once, his frame coiling. "*Ange*, what?"

"That face…"

"Which face? Where?"

Hal shook her head once, her mind spinning between memories spanning years of missions and the moment of seven heartbeats ago.

She never forgot a face or a drawing, but placing them…

"Thirteen people from the stair's entrance," she recited, clarity snapping into place. "On your left. Tall. Light hair. Angular face, but sunken. Frowning, disapproving, bored. Dark coat, blue waistcoat, ridiculous cravat."

Pratt took a long, slow glance about the room, starting with everyone and anyone to their right before panning to look behind them. "I see him," he told her as he came back to center. "Who?"

"Don't know," she ground out, inching closer, her smile paining her face. "But I've drawn him, John. I've *drawn* him."

The slow intake of breath told her that her husband understood the significance of that statement and took it seriously.

"Where?" Hal hissed to herself. "Where?"

Pratt's free hand came to rest on hers, firm yet gentle, his hold secure. "Calm yourself. We are not under any pressure constrained to a timeline, and your exacting mind is not going to work any better with you forcing it. Smile."

"Smile?" Hal couldn't believe her ears. How in the world was she supposed to smile when someone who had been somehow part of an investigation was in this same building?

"Smile, *Ange*," Pratt ordered, squeezing her hand. "Breathe. Walk. Let your mind work, and give it the space to do so."

Her teeth ground together, her jaw ached, resistance and rebellion against instruction rising like a tide she couldn't hold back.

If she could just go back. Demand to speak with that face. Put all the pieces together until something emerged from them.

"*Ange*," Pratt said again, this time with surprising gentleness. "Inhale."

She did so, completely against her will, the action surprising her.

"Exhale."

The air in her lungs expelled on cue, somehow not rendering her into a pathetic, panting, embarrassing excuse for a woman supposedly of high standing with well-connected relations.

"And again."

This time, she allowed herself to do so with intention, the panic beginning to fade, and the pressure. With those obstacles removed, the whirl of faces slowed and came into better focus.

How infuriating. Her husband was right.

"I hate you," Hal muttered half-heartedly as she eased against Pratt, letting him lead her in following the others.

"Only because it worked," he pointed out with a smile. "You've given us our first clue in this puzzle, and now we have to work it out. Perhaps the opera will jog something in your memory."

She sniffed with a hint of derision. "And now he smiles."

"Of course." Pratt seemed to stride a bit more proudly, his posture much improved. "You've made the entire evening far more enjoyable for me with a simple stroke of your brilliance."

Hal looked up at him, her eyes narrowing. "Did you just compliment me?"

Pratt glanced down at her, half-smile still in place. "Out of all that I've said, *that* is what impressed you most?"

"It's such a rarity, I had to be certain I wasn't imagining it." She smiled and drummed her fingers along his arm. "Brilliance, you say. Hmm. What a novelty, I'd never considered such a thing."

"Now, don't wave your butterfly net about for more compliments," Pratt teased as he led them into the box after her cousin, leaning close enough that his lips brushed the rim of her ear. "I have so few to give for anyone, I cannot, in all conscience, exceed those limits for you."

Hal nodded soberly, warmth spreading from the center of her chest throughout her body with every continuing beat of her heart, though the skin of her ear continued to buzz in a ticklish manner.

"Of course."

"But brilliance, *Ange*," he said again, his voice lowering in both volume and timbre. "Absolute brilliance."

If he said that word one more time, she would either laugh, blush, punch him, or kiss him.

And she wasn't sure which reaction she would succumb to.

"Indeed, Monsieur Pratt," de Rouvroy agreed in an almost booming voice, making Hal jump as Pratt assisted her to her seat. "It is a piece of complete brilliance, is it not? Such a beautiful building, and not half so grand as the *Salle le Peletier*, if you can believe that."

Hal snickered behind a hand when she caught Pratt's miserable expression as he sat beside her. "Save me," Pratt whispered. "Find your familiar face, I beg you."

"I don't know," Hal mused with a flutter of her lashes, opening her fan and setting it to work in as elegant a manner as possible. "I'm rather enjoying this discussion of architecture and art and decor…"

"*Ange*…" He gave her a long-suffering look. "Please."

Shaking her head, she reached out to pat his arm, leaving her hand there as she scanned the other guests taking their seats.

"Anything?" Pratt asked eagerly.

"In the last fifteen seconds?" she shot back. "Not bloody likely. Have you seen the number of people here?"

He held up his free hand in a sign of surrender. "Apologies. Please." He gestured to the theatre with a sigh. "We have… a long time."

Hal nodded as she continued to look, seeking the flash of the familiar she had felt and seen earlier. The overture of the opera began, and still she looked, hoping she was no longer the subject of inspection for others, as her attention was anywhere but on the stage.

The actors began to perform, when finally, she found the face she sought.

She smiled indulgently and leaned closer to her husband, her fingers sliding down his arm until her fingers laced between his.

He jerked beside her, but quickly recovered, leaning towards her in expectation.

Intelligent man.

"Last box across from us," she whispered. "Towards the center. Third seat in, second row."

"Bless smaller theatres," he replied in the same tone.

Again, Hal nodded, the motion brushing her hair against him, which she somehow felt to her toes. "See him?"

This time he nodded. "I do. Try to recollect the specifics of how you know him. Leave the interval to me."

"The interval?" Hal hissed, facing him more fully. "What are you…?"

He gave her a quelling look, somehow smiling without smiling. "Leave it to me," he said again.

Scowling, Hal nudged him hard, but let her attention move to the stage, then promptly fix itself on her memories, sketch after sketch flipping through her mind.

She would find the man. She would remember who had seen him. She would be able to tie him to their mission somehow.

She would.

As if he could hear her thoughts, feel her determination, Pratt's fingers, still laced between hers, curved around her own, comfort and confidence tight in their grasp.

Chapter Seven

"I don't see why I couldn't have come with you. To be left in the box with Victoire and Agathe was torture, I'll have you know."

"I'm sure it was."

"What in the world do you mean by that?"

John exhaled in resignation and looked across the small table in the parlor he and Hal shared while they ate their breakfast. Thankfully, de Rouvroy and his family were not so particular about breakfast that they had everyone eat it together in the breakfast room at a particular hour. René and de Rouvroy ate there themselves, naturally, and the children did as well, but it happened that Madame de Rouvroy and Agathe were more inclined to take trays.

He'd been hard-pressed not to kiss their host's feet when he'd suggested that they also might enjoy breakfast in their rooms, though he could have done without the mischievous smile that had accompanied it.

Whatever the reason, solitary breakfast with his partner was a blessed relief.

Most of the time.

"You don't engage in small talk, Hal," he explained, ignoring how she had yet to put her hair up and it waved down her neck and across her shoulders with a freedom that intrigued him. "This isn't a flaw; or, if it is, then it is one we share. Even with ladies as admirable as Madame de Rouvroy and as fine as Agathe…"

"She's not *that* fine," Hal grumbled with an impressive frown as she picked up her coffee. "Surly, spoiled brat. I'll wager you half a crown she marries an aged marquis with a gouty disposition near to reclining on his deathbed and weasels the whole of his fortune away from his legitimate heirs."

John blinked at the specificity of her suggestion and actually paused in the middle of his point. "Is that half a crown for that exact result? Or for each aspect of it?"

The look his wife gave him would have made her a widow, albeit not an especially wealthy one.

More's the pity.

"At any rate," he went on quickly, "I'll take your wager, and furthermore, you'd have hated being up and about with René, de Rouvroy, and myself just the same."

"I highly doubt that." She sipped her coffee slowly, and John felt the almost bitter taste of the beverage in his own mouth, wondering how in the world she could drink it. "Walking about in silence would have been an improvement on the situation, let alone having intelligent conversation."

John shook his head and buttered the dry toast before him. "Nothing intelligent about it. Your cousin and his son, bless them, are worse than any sixteen-year-old girls I have ever met. They knew everyone and had to chat with everyone. They were energized by each conversation and dragged me from person to person as though I were a pawn in a social game of chess."

"Who won?" Hal murmured, eyeing him with a smile over her cup.

"Amusing." He cleared his throat. "I had to meet nearly every person in attendance purely so I could meet the one man I wished to."

Hal's eyes widened and her throat moved on a swallow as she set her cup down. "You met him? Why didn't you say anything last night?"

He raised a brow at her. "How could I? René insisted on riding with us and chatted the whole way home. You did your best to give him the right impression, scowling every time he asked a question about England, even if he is too simple minded to have noticed."

"That's a bit harsh," she scolded, though there was no force behind her tone.

"He isn't simple in the mind," John told her, rolling his eyes. "He's only filled the space with more fluff than he should and thus has no room for weighty matters. Even you can admit that."

She nodded as she spun her teacup on its saucer. "Of course I can. I only felt the need to defend him as my relation. So René prevented the revelation last night, but it's not as though he shares rooms with us. Why not tell me then?"

"Because I was deuced tired, and so were you, and nothing could have been done last night. Now, would you like to know or not?"

Hal gestured quickly, sitting forward in her chair eagerly.

"Monsieur Laurent Fontaine," John told her with a small smile. "Influential, wealthy, stately, but all in all, none too impressive. Showed absolutely no inclination to be friendly to de Rouvroy or René, though he took no pains to discourage them from conversation."

"Did he react at all to your name?" Hal demanded. "Did he seem familiar to you at all? Did he recognize you?"

"No, no, and no." He let his smile spread as he bit into his toast and cut into a piece of ham. "You are the only one between us who suspects him, for which I thank you. Any details come to you yet?"

Hal sat back in her chair roughly, pursing her lips. "Sort of. It was one of Gent's faces, and I think it was from a party. The trouble is that he does so many of them and I've drawn so many faces for him that I cannot place him in particular. I don't suppose it matters, though." She smiled ruefully and plucked a piece of toast from her plate, taking a quick bite. "I never have the details of their assignments when I make the drawings, so we really are no worse off than I ever am."

No, they were not, and they had, in fact, gotten further than John would have expected to at this stage. They hadn't even been in Paris for a week and they already had a lead to investigate. They might not know how exactly he was tied in, or what he might be suspected of, but any person, male or female, whom Hal had drawn for an operative was worth pursuing.

There was some question as to how exactly they could investigate Monsieur Fontaine, but a sociable host would certainly be a benefit in that regard.

Unfortunate for John, but a benefit for the mission.

That would undoubtedly become a pattern.

A knock sounded at their parlor door, and they glanced at each other in confusion. As a general rule, they were not disturbed here, which was part of the attraction in remaining within.

"Come," Hal called, shrugging her shoulders, eyes widening.

One of the footmen entered, the brilliant blue and gold of his livery almost startling in its shade against the relative simplicity of the parlor. "*Monsieur et madame, un message por vous, s'il vous plaît.*"

"*Merci,*" John murmured as he reached for the note on the platter.

The footman gave a crisp nod, clicked his heels, and left the parlor with nearly silent steps.

"A note?" Hal frowned at the paper in John's hand as he broke the seal. "Who in the world knows we are here?"

"Our brothers," John reminded her, laughing once.

"Ugh." Hal rolled her eyes. "They wouldn't write to us, and you know it."

John nodded as he scanned the message. "Why would Madame Moreau send us a note to thank us for our patronage?"

Hal blinked. "I haven't the faintest idea. She did?"

"And in English, too." He frowned and tilted his head for a moment. "Not particularly accomplished English, but English still."

"She spoke it well enough, what do you mean?"

He pointed at a passage and showed it to her. "See here? The sentence structure is backwards, and it would be wrong in French, too. Strange, isn't it?"

Hal tapped on a word near the bottom. "Pratt. She hopes I am enjoying my parasol?"

"Yes. So?"

His wife scooted her chair closer, which forced him to look at her, the proximity not as startling as it was enticing.

His eyes wanted to drift to her lips, but he forced them to remain where they were, though every motion of those lips was noticed in periphery.

"I didn't get a parasol from Madame Moreau."

The hypnotic motion, even in limited view, repeated itself in his mind's eye at least four times before the words those lips had said caused his actual eyes to blink, breaking the spell.

"You didn't?" He looked back to the message with far more interest. "That is exceptionally interesting…"

Hal scooted closer, her attention on the paper as well. "What does it mean, Pratt?"

"Not sure." He tilted the paper this way and then that, letting the light play on it, his pulse skittering with familiar excitement and anticipation. "Well, well… Let's see what this little pretty has to say."

"Are you going to turn into an obsessive paramour with a certain degree of lewdness over a note? Because if you are…"

"Don't be ridiculous," John breathed as his eyes danced over every letter in every word, flew across the page with a scrutiny that should not have matched the speed. "Nothing lewd about it. Full, healthy, dedicated appreciation is more appropriate. It's an experience, you see. Revealing the truth beneath what is before you, not exposing it. Nothing is as it seems, or means what it says, and everything you've assumed is absolutely irrelevant until you discover that beauty hidden from eyes that know not what they see."

A soft scoffing sound near his left ear made him smile despite his search. "And now you've turned poet and philosopher as well as patron. I barely recognize you."

"Shh," he said softly as his eyes darted to and fro. "I'm almost there."

"Are you really?" Her voice was stunned, disbelieving, and, he flattered himself, impressed. "How?"

He shook his head very slightly, patterns forming. "In a moment, *Ange*. Just wait…"

She heeded him now, and only the faint ticking of a mantle clock accompanied his work. He could feel her hovering around his arm, sense her efforts to see what he was, knew she was waiting for some answer from him, any answer at all. In his usual work, such observant company would have detracted from his efficacy, perturbed his process into something he couldn't tolerate.

Not this time.

Not with her.

"There."

The word surprised him as he said it, and a heartbeat later he nodded, seeing now what his mind acknowledged before his eyes did.

"There," he said again. "Fetch me another piece of paper, will you?"

She was already handing him one before he finished the request, and he looked at it, then up at her in puzzled surprise.

"What?" Hal lifted a shoulder in a half-shrug as she took her chair again. "I knew you had it from the first 'there.' Seemed to me you'd want to take it down, so I didn't see the need to wait for the invitation."

"I'll make a note of that for future reference." He flashed her a quick smile and returned to the note. "Right. Let's see what you really say, pet."

"Do you always talk to your puzzles?" Hal teased, leaning an elbow on the table.

"Only if it needs the encouragement." He squinted for a moment, then started writing down the letters in question. "But it seems she's in a giving mood."

Hal grunted once. "Good for her. Care to share?"

John nodded and showed her the page of letters he'd written, biting back a laugh.

She stared at it, then gave him a dark look. "What does it *really* say?"

"Exactly what I wrote. Look." He set the paper down and began to divide the jumble into words with slashes between the letters. "We are trained to only read things in a certain format. Change the format, and you change the significance. You see?" He slid the paper to her again, this time his smile for her nod.

"Yes, I do. But who are we to meet in Place Royale by the third tree to the west?" She glanced up, a furrow between her fair brows. "Surely, not Madame Moreau herself."

John shook his head and sat back. "Not likely. Weaver did say we would have contacts here, and they would make themselves known. This is likely one of them. We know we can trust Madame Moreau, so I have no reason to suspect a trap."

Hal nodded, then picked up the original note and compared it to the translation John had written. "Pratt."

"Hal?"

"How the bloody hell did you see this in that?" She rustled the pages in turn for emphasis, slouching forward in unladylike fashion as she studied them. "There is no possible way to know where the message was in all of that in the time you accomplished this."

John chuckled and folded his arms, taking a selfish moment to feel quite proud of himself. "Of course it's possible. I just did it."

The papers hit the table beneath pressing palms, the sound of the thumping echoing almost ominously, despite the diminutive size of the table itself. "So help me, Pratt, I will throttle you in ways they don't teach at the Convent or anywhere else."

"I'm afraid to ask." He sat up and rested an arm on the table, flicking his fingers at the letter. "This is what I'm trained to do, Hal. I search for patterns, for hints, for anomalies… Especially anomalies, because that's usually where I start to get somewhere. Anything that doesn't fit is suspicious. How do I do it at the speed I do? Practice. And it's not always fast, I can assure you. This one was fairly simple compared to other projects I've had."

Hal twisted her lips, the furrow between her brows deepening. "Teach me."

John's eyes shot to her face, though her attention was still on the letter. There was something about the determined set of her jaw and the way it contrasted with the fullness of her cheeks that fascinated him, to say nothing of the faintest pink hue right at the place where jaw and cheekbone united. Something about the simplicity of her look this morning that he admired, and the unadorned air about her that he welcomed. Would have encouraged.

Wanted to keep.

He swallowed and returned his attention to the letter. "All right," he murmured, clearing his throat. "Take a look at the original letter again. Look for patterns, hints, and…?"

"Anomalies." Hal nodded and bit her lip as her eyes scanned.

He could barely see her do so, but he felt the teeth on that lip as though it were his own.

Perhaps he needed to drink coffee in the mornings, too. Clearly, he was not functioning well.

"Here," Hal said at last, pointing at a word. "Parasol. We know that didn't happen, so it clearly doesn't fit."

John nodded once. "Very good. So, if we look at that…"

An hour later, the first lesson complete, the pair of them strolled along the paths in Place Royale with other fashionable members of Paris Society, ambling aimlessly as they all were in high finery that would never have been seen outside of a ballroom in London.

Aimless ambling had never sat well with John, nor would it ever.

But without an identity to their contact, there was nothing else to do until they reached the third tree to the west. What were they to do by that tree without making it obvious that they were waiting?

"How are we supposed to meet our contact in such a popular park in the middle of the day?" Hal hissed as they walked.

"I have no idea," John replied. "I leave that to the actual spies."

He would swear later he could hear his wife scowl. "Clever, Pratt. So very clever."

"I try."

Really, he just couldn't help himself; the witty quips seemed to just fly from his lips around her even when he knew it would irritate her.

Especially when he knew it would irritate her.

The Shopkeepers would be searching for his body one of these days. They would never find it.

They reached the tree in question, and Hal made a show of resting beneath its shade, as any proper lady would, while John stood by and observed their surroundings as any polite but bored gentleman would.

And they waited.

"Isn't this lovely?" Hal grumbled after a few minutes. "We should have our portraits painted thusly."

"Just because you haven't spent much time out of doors in the last fifteen years does not mean the outdoors are an evil," John pointed out calmly. "Breathe in the fresh air."

"There is no fresh air to be had in Paris, you dolt. And if you've seen the sun outside of a window for more than ten minutes at a time since the age of twelve, I will eat these lace gloves." She made an indignant huff and looked away. "Impossible man."

John smirked and continued to look where he would in an attempt to spot their contact.

"*Excusez-moi, monsieur... Des pièces à épargner?*" a gravelly voice from his right.

"*Non,*" John said quickly, stepping back even as he turned to face the old beggar. "*Je suis désolé...*"

A grunt emanated from the beggar. "Thought not. Englishmen are always cheap."

The clarity of the pure English tone would have dropped John's jaw had he not spent years practicing locking it in place. "*Ange.* Have you any coins in your reticule?"

Hal was beside him in a moment, her fingers digging into the beaded pouch. "Oh, I think so. Let me see..."

"Call me *Ruse,*" the man said in a low tone, the croaking aspect from before vanishing completely. "Welcome to Paris."

"Oh, bother, I could have sworn..." Hal said aloud without raising her voice in an obvious manner, her hand still fumbling within her reticule, her eyes on their companion.

He nodded at her in acknowledgment. "An invitation will arrive for you both this afternoon for an evening engagement tomorrow. You will accept, and your relations will also be pleased to do so. It would behoove you to make the acquaintance of Monsieur Leclerc, and to welcome any closer association."

"No, *Ange,*" John said out of instinct, "that is too much."

"Quite right," she replied, jingling her reticule further.

"Leclerc cannot be trusted," Ruse went on. "But he will be useful. We have reason to believe he is a courier of sorts, so if you can do something there..."

"Leave it to me," Hal murmured in an almost dark, satisfied tone.

Ruse surprised them by grinning. "Trick hinted you might like that. He sends his regards, by the way."

Hal only offered a low laugh in response.

John wasn't sure what she meant by that.

"Above all else, be discreet." Ruse looked between the two of them severely. "Trust no one. No one is what they seem in France these days." He flashed another quick grin. "Yours truly aside."

"That should do it, no?" Hal fished a coin from her reticule and handed it over, carefully avoiding touching the dirty palm. "How do we contact you?" she asked in a much softer tone.

Ruse's lips twisted to one side. "Place a single candle in your parlor window."

"You have us under surveillance?" John asked, his brows shooting up.

"Oh, Sphinx." Ruse laughed darkly. "You have no idea where we are and just how closely we lurk. This is a crucial mission, and none of us are willing to risk failure." His fingers closed around the coin Hal had given him. "*Merci beaucoup, madame. Dieu vous bénissez.*"

"*Vous aussi,*" Hal replied, but their only known contact was already shuffling away, his gait staggering to the left, stumbling as other patrons of the park took pains to avoid him.

John watched him go, then offered an arm to his wife. "Well, *Ange,*" he sighed, "shall we venture back?"

"Let's walk a few moments more," she suggested softly, her hand curving around his upper arm as if for protection. "There is a great deal more to think about now."

John nodded in agreement and exhaled slowly as they left the shade of the tree, thoughts awhirl. "The sun and air will do us both good."

Hal prodded his side hard with her elbow, and he smiled at the pressure.

Chapter Eight

"It is *extraordinaire* that you have already received an invitation since you've been here. Marvelous! Did we meet Monsieur Savatier at the theatre? I must have made the introduction, indeed I must. Lovely family, beautiful wife, and quite respectable by any standards. He was a soldier for the emperor, you know, though we mustn't admire such things now. But he is favored of His Majesty, so we must admire that. This will set you both up in Paris, I am sure of it. Do you like cards, Pratt? There is destined to be excellent French wine at Savatier's, you can be sure, and cards and wine are an excellent pairing."

"Do you think he expects me to react or reply at any time?" Pratt asked Hal softly, leaning close while her cousin continued to prattle on about everything and nothing.

Hal clamped down on her bottom lip to stifle a giggle. "Not really. He must be eager to attend tonight."

Pratt grunted once. "Well, he is making me less so with his excessive enthusiasm. Make it stop."

"Shh!" She gave him a scolding smile. "We have to pretend tonight. You know that."

"I don't see why I have to pretend I enjoy being social," Pratt muttered. "I'm already pretending far too much."

Something about that statement stiffened Hal's spine and made her shift uncomfortably. Was that a note of bitterness she heard in his voice? What else was he pretending that he could possibly resent?

The opera hadn't been terrible, and they had started to find details for their mission there. They were remarkably relaxed at her cousin's home, never had to stand on ceremony, and were left to themselves for the most part. The children ran amok with regularity but rarely got in their way.

What was he pretending there?

Was he pretending with her?

The thought sent her gnawing on the inside of her cheek, anxiety and insecurity warring within her, and soon her own resentment joined in. They had only spoken about the mission and details, never about anything particularly personal, and unless he was bitter about being married to her for the time being, the only thing he might have pretended at was cordiality with her.

If that bothered him, there were bigger problems than their mission lying under the surface.

She wasn't pretending at cordiality with him. She wasn't pretending when she asked to learn about finding the code in the letter. She wasn't pretending in her determination to accomplish their mission.

She wasn't pretending at all when it came to him.

Was she wrong? Should she have been more guarded with him? With the mission? Should she have been pretending and protecting herself constantly?

Perhaps this was why she hadn't been selected for operations at the Convent. She wasn't an operative at heart, and she wasn't an operative by nature.

That was hardly the mentality she needed at this moment, considering the carriage was just pulling up to their destination wherein she would have to pretend to be a British *émigré* without drawing any attention while pretending to be one.

Lovely.

"Ah, yes," her cousin said, puffing his chest out as he moved for the door. "You will be impressed, I think. Come, come."

Hal looked across the carriage at Victoire, who seemed almost exasperated by her husband. "Forgive him, please," she pleaded with a laugh in her sweetly accented voice. "He feels so alive around other people."

"You don't feel the same way?" Hal asked, tilting her head ever so slightly.

Victoire sighed as she scooted to the edge of her seat, preparing to leave the carriage. "I much prefer a quiet evening at home. Ah well. Perhaps one day." She offered a fleeting smile, then took her husband's hand and exited.

"Not any time soon, unfortunately," Pratt murmured with some sympathy. "Not with her children. Well, shall we?"

Hal scowled as Pratt moved out of the carriage and offered a hand to her. "No need to be so cheery. Really, one will mistake you for the sun."

Pratt's furrowed brow would have made her scowl further had the others not been watching. "What are you talking about?"

"Never you mind," she huffed as she took his hand and stepped down. With a smile entirely for the benefit of Jean and Victoire, Hal gripped her husband's elbow. "Lead on, cousin."

Needing no further encouragement, Jean did so, chattering away as he had before, while Hal and Pratt followed.

"Are you nervous?" Pratt asked in a quiet tone. "You seem a bit abrupt."

"Perhaps that's just my nature finally in full effect," Hal snapped. She exhaled shortly through her nose, trying to force a calm she did not feel. "No, I am not nervous. The idea of pretending has me irritable."

That, at least, was true, and he could take it for what he would. There was no need to elaborate or expound, and she could have some relief in speaking her mind, even if it was not in full.

He'd never know.

"I can understand that." He sighed heavily and shook his head. "We're not field operatives, you and I. But we need not pretend too far out of our nature. The only real pretending would be our opinions on England, if we are able to express them, right?"

Was that all he thought they were pretending? All he thought she was talking about?

Intriguing.

"I suppose," she said slowly, doing her best not to look up at him.

He nodded as though he hadn't heard her response. "We would never be able to maintain the subterfuge of pretended characteristics of our natures with the same continuity regardless of the audience. So why not be ourselves?"

"Because we are not actually a married couple?" Hal quipped before she could help herself.

Pratt stopped her and gave her a serious look, one brow rising. "I beg your pardon, *Ange*. I think you will find that we *are* married, and certain individuals went to great pains to bring that about. The fact that neither you nor I were particularly thrilled by those pains is irrelevant now."

Hal made a face, some of the tension leaving her spine as she looked down at the tips of her slippers.

"I suppose," she replied again, this time with reluctant acceptance.

Pratt pressed two fingers beneath her chin and tipped her face up towards his. "*Ange*, we may not have gotten along in the past, but I'd like to think that, in the last few days, we've become friends, at least. If that's true, we're certainly among the rarity in British Society. Surely, we don't have to pretend that there is, in part, some affection in our marriage."

There was nothing to do but sigh very softly at that, and Hal allowed herself to smile up at him. "No, John," she admitted, loving the smile she received at the use of his given name. "No, we don't have to pretend that."

His eyes searched hers for a moment, even in the fading light of evening, as though he were deciphering the code written there, and then he nodded, his smile still in place. "Then I suppose we need not pretend much at all."

Hal grinned without reservation, her heart feeling lighter than it had since leaving London. "Apparently not."

"*Mes cousins, vous venez?*" Jean called, waiting for them just outside the door to Monsieur Savatier's home.

"Oui, oui, nous arrivons," Pratt replied as he winked at Hal and dropped his hand from her chin, leaving the skin almost chilled in his absence.

They turned and hurried to follow, Hall pulling herself closer to her husband than she had done before.

"What did Ruse mean when he suggested you could do something with Leclerc's potential role?" Pratt hissed while they were still out of earshot of the others.

Hal smiled slyly up at him. "One of the skills I did manage to acquire in my life that would have served me well is the ability to pick a pocket without detection. Very few people know that, including my dear, devoted godfather."

Pratt barked a laugh and shook his head. "Of course you can. Well, well, *Ange*, perhaps tonight will be entirely devoted to you."

"Perhaps it will." She shrugged a shoulder as though it was possible, if not entirely plausible. "I'm sure you'll find some useful occupation for the evening."

"Impudent, wife."

"Thank you, husband."

Pratt nudged her side gently in response, and Hal could have beamed the entire night because of it.

But there was work to be done, and despite their teasing, they would both need to take part.

The home of Monsieur Savatier was an immaculate one and held none of the excesses that Jean and Victoire's house did. Clean, elegant, simple, and, in a way, celebrating the natural features of the house rather than using them as avenues for decor.

Hal liked him already, or perhaps it was his wife that held such taste. Either way, she approved of their taste and style and felt far more comfortable here than she had at any point in her cousin's grander residence. There would not be much pretending at all in her compliments for their host and hostess, and something about that, considering what they were about here, made her smile in complete irony.

"What's the smile for?" Pratt asked softly as they made their way up the stairs to the entertaining rooms.

"I like this house," she whispered back. "It's lovely, isn't it?"

Pratt seemed to exhale a laugh. "My thoughts, as well. It will be interesting to discover what Savatier's fortune is, considering he doesn't seem to live as though he has one."

"Is it wrong to approve of someone we may be investigating?"

Hal asked in an even softer voice, the words barely audible even to her own ears.

"We have no idea if he is involved yet," her husband replied, his lips just above her ear. "Approve of whom and what you will, we only need information."

"Ah, sweet nothings between hearts bound together," Jean said from the top of the stairs, looking back at them with a warm smile. "Early days of marriage are *très sucré*, are they not?"

Hal glanced up at John, biting back a laugh, only to find him doing the same. She looked back at her cousin with a smile. "Indeed, cousin."

Jean chuckled and gestured for them to enter the room ahead of him and Victoire.

The drawing room was expansive, simply adorned as the rest of the house, and full of people without being a crush. The fashions Hal observed in the ladies were middling in their finery, placing Hal's ensemble in line with them, though the additional adornments in her hair, placed at the insistence of her maid, were more excessive than the rest. One could not have everything, she supposed.

"Baron de Rouvroy," an elegant woman in palest blue greeted with a warm smile, a hint of rouge on her cheeks.

Jean stepped forward and took her hand, kissing the glove quickly. "Madame Savatier. Thank you for the kind invitation. I pray you will excuse my using English, *ma cousine* and her husband, Monsieur Pratt, are English." He gestured to them.

Madam Savatier offered them both a bright smile, though she raised a brow. "And you have no confidence in your French?" she asked with only a hint of her natural accent.

Hal curtseyed in greeting. "*J'ai confiance en mon français, madame, mais pas assez de compétence.*"

"And I have no confidence at all, I'm afraid," Pratt sighed, putting even more of an emphasis on his English accent than usual. "All the more reason to let my wife speak for us both."

Madam Savatier giggled and shook her head. "*Non*, it is no trouble to speak in your native tongue, Monsieur Pratt. Welcome to our home. It is a pleasure to have you."

"And a pleasure to be here," Hal replied, finding Madame

Savatier relatively without airs and instantly liking her. "We were surprised and delighted to have the invitation."

"I would expect so," Madame Savatier laughed. "My husband will insist upon inviting any new acquaintances to our home for further engagement. Sometimes it leads to nothing, but other times we gain marvelous new friends!" She laughed, then looked among the group and returned her attention to Jean. "Your son is not with you?"

"Alas, madame," Jean replied sadly, "he has a prior engagement this evening. He sends his regards and his regrets."

Madame Savatier dipped her chin in a nod. "All is forgiven, of course." She gestured to the room in invitation. "Please enjoy yourselves. I shall come along *bientôt* to introduce you to some new friends, Madame Pratt."

Hal managed a smile, though she hoped that it would not be too soon. Unless Madam Savatier was going to introduce her to Leclerc, she had other things to see to.

"*Merci*," she replied all the same.

Pratt led her away and they shared a look with Jean and Victoire.

"Go on, *mes enfants*," he insisted in a teasing, fatherly tone. "Do not wait for me to take you about. I intend to spend this evening with my wife." He kissed her hand as though to prove it.

"Better and better," Pratt muttered as they walked away. He exhaled and gave Hal a look. "Ready?"

She nodded at him, her heart skipping with anticipation. "Ready."

"If we need the other," he suddenly said, his eyes growing dark, "what shall we do?"

Hal thought quickly. "I'll fiddle with my necklace, you your cravat. As you hate it anyway, it will not be at all surprising."

Pratt glowered at the offending linen darkly. "It's more voluminous than your skirts."

"Very pretty, though." She winked and tugged him in the direction of some other guests.

The very first question after introductions were made was all too perfect, in Hal's estimation. "And what brings you to Paris, Madame Pratt? The fashions?"

Hal smiled at the tall man who had asked. "My family, monsieur.

I had never met my cousin, Baron de Rouvroy, and I wished to rekindle the connection my mother abandoned."

"Abandoned?" one of the ladies repeated, struggling to say the word in English. "How?"

"She chose to follow her heart and married my father," Hal continued, "for which I am obviously grateful, but she severed anything French from her life and devoted herself to England. Not that her devotion was rewarded." She let herself frown, then brightened. "But with my recent marriage to Mr. Pratt here, who shares my desire to embrace France, I was able to come and restore the connection."

Some in the group shared confused looks and Hal wondered if she had gone too far. She hadn't said much beyond the truth, even if her emphasis was enhanced for effect.

"You do not love England, then?" one of the men asked.

Hal pretended to consider that. "I suppose I do, as it is the land of my birth, but I fear that love has become tinged with bitterness. My brother has been made an outcast for his views in life, my parents were never mourned in their deaths, and I have no tolerance for the airs Society seems to have taken upon themselves." She smiled for the effect of the group. "England is not as perfect as they like to pretend, I fear."

"Neither is France," another man assured her, bringing laughter from the group.

"The King has done nobody good," the tall man from before insisted. "He rules as though it is the year 800 rather than 1825. Returning to excesses is all he has done, and the country does not need such things."

"No indeed," Pratt agreed, entering the conversation for the first time. "He is quite unlike his brother, the late king, is he not?"

A general discussion of the monarchy and differences between them ensued, and it was made perfectly clear that Charles, the present French monarch, was wildly unpopular. His predecessor received a fair enough opinion, all things considered, but nothing particularly glowing.

There was no mention of the emperor or anything surrounding him.

That wasn't surprising, but there wasn't anything anyone had said that would leave Hal suspicious of Faction patronage.

Still, word would spread that the Pratts weren't satisfied with England, and that could be enough.

She hoped.

"Monsieur Pratt, are you a man of cards?" the tall man asked.

"I can be persuaded," Pratt replied, smiling beyond mere politeness. "Lead on."

He nodded at Hal as he left, and the gentlemen of their little gathering all seemed to follow, leaving her alone with the ladies.

"You have a remarkably handsome husband, Madame Pratt," one of the ladies confessed, fanning herself with a little more intensity. "*Très charmant*."

Hal felt her cheeks coloring in an instant, which made the others laugh.

"*Merci*," she replied softly. "I do believe I have chosen well."

"*C'est vrai*!" another insisted.

"Madame Pratt, come," Madame Savatier suddenly said, coming to her side and taking an arm. "I must show you off." She nodded to the others and steered Hal away expertly. "They will contrive to take your husband away from your bed," she told Hal softly. "They always do. Dissatisfaction with their own husbands and general boredom leads to unfortunate behavior. This group will suit much better for you."

"Thank you," Hal told her with utter sincerity, fighting the urge to look back at the ladies and glare with the power of a thousand daggers.

Madam Savatier patted her hand. "*Pas du tout*, *ma chère*." She quickly introduced Hal to the new group and indicated the man to her right. "I will leave you in the care of Monsieur Leclerc, madame. He is very respectable and will ensure that Monsieur Pratt will return to find his wife safe and among friends."

"Such responsibility," Leclerc joked from beside her, shaking his head. "Madame Savatier, you put so much trust in me."

She gave him a severe look. "Do not prove me false, Leclerc. Mademoiselle Favreau would not appreciate the discovery that her intended is not respectable."

Leclerc bowed in acknowledgement. "*Au revoir*, madame."

Hal watched their hostess leave and smiled at the gathering she had joined. "I hope you do not mind an Englishwoman joining you."

"Of course not," the woman beside her exclaimed in perfect English, a hand going to Hal's arm. "You dress like a French woman, which is more than I can say for other ladies of your country I have met. This is simply *charmante*."

"Thank you," Hal told her with a smile. "I had Madame Moreau prepare my wedding trousseau."

That earned her a round of approving nods, and a discussion of recent fashion began, the gentlemen engaging just as much as the ladies, to her surprise.

"You do not think a gentleman has as much interest in his apparel as a woman?" Leclerc asked her in a low voice.

Hal blushed at being caught in her thoughts. "Am I so obvious?"

Leclerc chuckled and shook his head. "I know something of the English, madame, and it is no surprise to find your thoughts so."

"Have you been to England?"

"Several times. I find London fascinating, though lacking in the beauty Paris possesses." He looked down at her with a smile. "I hope this does not offend."

Hal smiled back easily. "Not at all. London has its charms, but I prefer the country."

"Ah." Leclerc turned towards her a little. "Which in particular? Do you have a country house, as so many do?"

"I am not so fortunate," Hal laughed, "nor so wealthy. No, my husband and I are in London for the present, though we will leave it as soon as we find something to our tastes. I adore the Lake District perhaps most of all. Have you seen it?"

"Sadly, no." Leclerc's eyes, dark and unreadable, seemed fixed on her with interest, though not the sort that would be considered flirtatious. It was rather the way Hal found herself looking at a drawing in progress, or how Pratt looked at the letter before the cipher was evident.

What did Leclerc think of Hal, and was she already suspected of something?

"You should see it," Hal told him when he did not say more. "It reminds me of the tales my mother told me of the south of France, though perhaps without the same pleasant weather."

Leclerc smiled at that and returned his attention to the group. "The south of France is quite picturesque to those who fail to see Paris for its beauty and its influence. I trust you will discover such while you are here."

"I do hope so." Hal felt her smile hardening. The change in Leclerc's tone and manner was fascinating considering their topic of discussion. "I find it rather diverting so far."

"I am glad of it." Leclerc sipped his wine slowly, laughing in response to something a member of their group had said.

Hal felt him losing interest, and she couldn't have that. She needed more opportunity, more conversation…

"Do you go to the opera, Monsieur Leclerc?" she tried with almost desperation.

He nodded, his eyes sliding to her again. "I do, in fact. A recent appreciation. Have you attended since your arrival in Paris?"

"We have. Just the other night, we saw *Elisabetta, regina d'Inghilterra.*" She held her breath, praying he would take advantage of the topic she had intentionally chosen.

"And what did you think of it?"

Exhaling, Hal let herself purse her lips in apparent thought. "I am English, monsieur. I have learned much about Queen Elizabeth in my life, and I grow weary of the topic. She did much good, I will allow, but she is revered almost as a saint, which history shows she was not. No monarch is. The opera itself was middling, and I found the whole affair rather tedious." Her eyes widened and she looked up at him in horror. "Please, monsieur, do not tell my cousin I said such things. He meant the experience to be a welcoming one for my husband and me, and I could not have him think…"

"Madame," Leclerc interrupted with some gentleness, his expression kind, "your secret will remain so, I promise."

"Thank you, monsieur." Hal shook her head, placing a hand on her cheek. "I am so ashamed. If you'll excuse me a moment, I will compose myself."

Leclerc nodded rather like a bow. "Of course, madame. I shall reserve your place beside me for when you return."

Hal smiled indulgently and moved away from him towards the window behind the group. Snapping open her fan, she began to move it steadily to bring cooler air to her complexion, though she doubted there was any color there to reduce.

Waiting a moment, she stared as though out of the window, though her attention was truly on the faint reflection in the glass rather than what lay beyond it.

Leclerc seemed to be watching her still, and she would not move until he was settled. His name was called by someone in the group, and he turned to address them, allowing Hal to move just slightly towards the corner, preventing her reflection from being clearly observed.

She slipped her hand into the hidden pocket in the folds of her skirts and quickly unfolded the paper she had deposited there only moments ago. She scanned every word on the page three times, committing each to memory, then refolded the note and returned it to her pocket, the fan still continuously moving in her free hand.

Tossing her head, she closed her eyes and exhaled to herself, and only for herself.

Then she turned with a smile and returned to the side of Leclerc as if nothing had occurred. "Thank you for indulging me."

He smiled as if her words amused him. "Nonsense, madame. Every lady is entitled to privacy to compose herself." He sipped his wine again before looking at her once more. "We were speaking of opera, yes?"

Hal nodded eagerly. "Yes. My cousin wishes to take us to more. Which would you recommend? My cousin is so easy, he loves so many of them."

Leclerc paused to think, though Hal suspected he did not need to. "There are several excellent operas in Paris at present. *La donna del lago*, if you wish to continue with Rossini, but you may enjoy Cherubini's *Les Abencérages* as well. It is not so popular as others, but sometimes those hidden treasures are *les meiux, non*?"

"*Oui*," Hal agreed, immediately adding the opera to her list. "And what of other events, Monsieur Leclerc? I am anxious to have friends in Paris."

"I don't think you will need to worry there, madame," he told her with a laugh. "I think friends will come to you." He gestured towards the door to the card room.

Pratt stood there, his eyes on Hal, interest evident, and there was no tugging at his cravat to call her to him.

She felt the pull all the same.

"That is my husband," Hal admitted, smiling without having to pretend anything at all.

"I see. Yes, the pair of you will do very well in Paris, I think." Leclerc chuckled again. "I should like to meet your husband, madame. Perhaps you can persuade him to come away from there?"

Hal hummed to herself, loving the connection she felt to the man smiling at her in a way that made her toes curl. "Perhaps I can, monsieur. *Excusez-moi.*" Without waiting for his response, Hal moved away, heading directly for Pratt where he stood.

"I didn't summon you," he murmured when she reached him, still smiling.

"I didn't need you to," she replied. "Were the cards not to your liking?"

Pratt shrugged. "Fair enough. The others are fetching stronger drinks, so I thought I'd see how you were."

Hal quirked her brows. "Well, if you can spare a moment, I have an introduction that is requested of you." She held out her hand to him, her heart leaping when he took it without hesitation.

"Indeed?" he asked as she squeezed his hand. "To whom am I being introduced?"

"Monsieur Leclerc."

His eyes widened, his smile spreading. "What luck. And did he meet your expectations?"

The unspoken message was clear, and Hal grinned. "Indeed, he did. Exceeded them, in fact. We'll discuss the details of it later."

Pratt nodded and surprised her by bringing the hand he held to his lips, kissing the back of it. "My brilliant *Ange*," he murmured. "Well done."

There was no mistaking the look in his eyes. He was not pretending this; she was not pretending the feelings she had.

They weren't pretending with each other. They couldn't be.

Which meant this was real.

"*Merci,* John," Hal whispered, her heart too full for further words.

His gentle smile would have made her sigh had they not been in public with work to continue.

"Come," she murmured, tugging on his hand. "You need to meet him."

"Yes, I suspect I do."

Chapter Nine

If only all things were as simple as one imagined they would be at the start, but then where would heaven and fate find their humor? Because it was clear that only heaven or fate could find humor in any of this. No one else would.

John couldn't.

He should have known that things were more complicated than they appeared; they wouldn't have brought him into this operation if things were simple. They wouldn't have brought Hal in if the players were all known to those important enough to have influence.

They wouldn't have brought either of them in if they could have intercepted, memorized, and decrypted these letters themselves. And if he'd forgotten that, the stack of letters before him would remind him, rather like a slap across the face.

He had nothing.

Absolutely nothing.

The letters were copies of the originals that Hal had picked and memorized, that mind of hers having far more ability than he'd ever expected. She copied them out for him the moment they returned home, and he'd begun to work on them.

He had yet to break a single one of them. Which made him a completely irrelevant asset to this mission. Hal could have done this on her own.

She *should* be doing this on her own.

He'd stay, of course, if for no other reason than to keep up the pretense of their marriage, and to ensure her safety, though he wasn't exactly a towering example of impressive musculature. He would assist her in any way he could, though at the present, that wouldn't be much at all.

How could he find nothing?

Six letters. Six in the space of two weeks, and nothing at all to show for it.

Every single cipher he could think of, he had applied to the letters. He'd looked at them individually, he'd looked at them collectively, he'd looked at them in batches… He'd even gone so far as to question Hal as to the accuracy of the words.

She had recited each and every letter verbatim without looking at them, then hadn't spoken to him for an entire day after that inquiry. In the tight quarters of their rooms, the silence had been deafening, and it had felt much, much longer.

He wouldn't be questioning her memory again, that was for certain.

But he didn't know what else to do. He hadn't struggled with a project like this in his career, had barely struggled in the years prior to beginning his career, and this was a crushing blow.

There would be no advantage for the Shopkeepers against the Faction if he couldn't break the cipher. There would be no regaining the ground lost in Rogue's compromise and Trace's capture. There would be no knowing what was planned, and every office that had operatives investigating the risk would be working half blind. It could very well be the fate of England herself in his hands.

And he had nothing.

John groaned and put his head in his hands, the pressure and the weight of such a responsibility seeming to pull him further and further into the earth, yet refusing to actually swallow him whole.

Yet another taste of the humor of heaven and fate. Hardly kind to him, but that was another matter.

"Still nothing?"

His wife's voice might have been the screech of an irritating rat for all the pleasure it gave him. He lifted his head and glared at her as she entered the parlor from her bedchamber.

"What do you mean by that?"

Any other woman might have stared back at him with wide eyes, surprised and hurt by the sharpness in his tone. They might have cried and made him feel an overwhelming sense of guilt for behaving badly. They might have fled the room in the face of their distress.

Not this woman. Not Henrietta Mortimer Pratt.

Not his *Ange*.

"Exactly what I said," she replied, somehow without actually snapping back, her hands going to her hips.

"If I had made any progress, I'd have informed you," he said, straightening his hair and folding his arms.

Hal snorted softly. "How magnanimous. What a noble partner I have."

The sarcasm stung as though each word were a blade, and his lip curled with the offense of it. "I don't need you reminding me of my failure, thank you very much. The throbbing ache ringing through my head on a semi-hourly basis is rather an apt reminder without your assistance."

As though the mention of it had bid its return, the now-familiar ache began between his eyes and spread up into the front of his head, pulsing ominously.

Hal stared at him without any emotion whatsoever. "If you're already declaring failure, we might as well go home."

"I'd love to."

"Marvelous. The Shopkeepers can find another artist with an exact memory and a codebreaker without equal, and *they* can marry for respectability and find connections in Paris on their own, hopefully with the right standing to get them the information that is needed so that every operative in England can feel a bit safer when they begin an assignment. I'm sure there's another pair ready to go at this moment."

"Shut up."

"No." This time she did snap at him and strode over to the table, leaning her hip against it and folding her arms to match his. "This is meant to be difficult, Pratt, or they could have brought in anyone else. Do you think I am the only person in the ranks who can draw with skill? Or the only person with an exemplary memory? Are you the only person any Shopkeeper knows who can decrypt and decipher messages?"

John didn't answer, instead, pinching the bridge of his nose in an attempt to stave off the pain.

"You have not failed," Hal insisted firmly. "You are being challenged, and that is all. When I ask if you still have nothing, I am not intimating that you ought to have found something by now. On the contrary, I am trying to be sympathetic to your evident discouragement. I am your *wife*, John, not your competition."

He swallowed at that, dropping his hand, unable to meet her eyes.

"I know," he whispered.

Hal waited, clearly expecting him to say more. When he did not, she sighed. "If you're going to be disagreeable about it, I'll take no more interest. Lord knows I've enough to be getting on with." She pushed away from the table and moved back towards her bedchamber, skirts swishing with the brisk strides that seemed to be her natural pace. "Blast these ridiculous petticoats," she muttered, making him smile despite his pain and melancholy.

The layers of additional fabric got in the way of how she preferred to walk, and even with practice and experience, she still had not grown accustomed to them.

Secretly, he hoped she never would.

"Hal," he called softly, not looking in her direction.

Her steps stopped, and he could almost hear her turn towards him. "Yes?"

"Why did you say wife?" He waited a beat, his fingers rubbing together with a sudden anxiety he didn't understand. "Why not partner instead?"

"Hmm." She took two steps in his direction. "I'm not sure. Is there a difference between them in our situation?"

John looked over at her, the clean lines of her gown and the simple style of her hair somehow presenting the most agreeable picture he'd ever seen her make. Not the most beautiful, but the most agreeable.

Most likeable.

Most comfortable.

"I suppose not," he replied, more to himself than anything else.

He half smiled and looked back at the letters, strangely not feeling guilt or shame about his outburst, though he couldn't say he approved of it. He'd had no recrimination from her, and it didn't appear to have caused her pain. On the contrary, she seemed to almost understand his frustration, and take it in perfect stride.

His own brother had never handled him so neatly.

"If you'd try coming back in here again in a moment or two, *Ange*," he told her simply, "I think you'll find a better-tempered husband sitting here."

"Oh, indeed?" came her bemused reply. "Could I find one with a larger fortune and darker hair while I am at it?"

He turned more fully towards his work, hiding the broader smile his lips had taken on. "I'm afraid not. Nor one with a particularly gifted singing voice, either."

She heaved a dramatic sigh. "That is a disappointment. One does hope for fulfillment of one's wishes in such things."

"Perhaps you should have married someone else," he suggested, holding his breath a moment.

"Oh, now, where would be the fun in that?" she asked in an almost bright tone. "Whatever would I do with a husband so very accommodating?" The swish of her skirts told him she had returned to the bedchamber, leaving him to grin like an idiot at the stack of impossible letters.

John shook his head, both at her wit and at his folly. "What, indeed?" he murmured to himself, pulling the top letter towards him without any hope for it at all.

It was some time before Hal ventured into the room again, and John had no progress to report to her when she did.

"I don't know what I'm missing, Hal," he confessed when she sat in the chair beside him. "I've tried every cipher I've seen used in Faction-related correspondence and codes. I've tried ciphers that were used in the war with America, on their side and ours. I've tried ancient ciphers and I've tried ciphers that most of the world hasn't seen yet. What they are using is either very sophisticated or very specific. Or both."

"Both?" Hal repeated, looking at the letter he was presently poring over. "How would someone do both?"

John sat back again with a sigh. "The Faction are overly cautious and layer their codes. You remember the trouble with Cap's family?"

She nodded insistently. "Of course. It was my letter from Trick that sent them to you in the first place."

"That gave us the hint about layers in the code," John confirmed. "It's time-consuming to decipher, but not impossible."

"Until now," Hal murmured with a hesitant glance at the letter.

He nodded. "Until now."

She frowned and turned towards him more fully. "How would you know that it's wrong or right? You'd have to decipher one way and then decipher those answers as well, over and over again until something worked, and that just couldn't be feasible."

"That's exactly how it works, in fact," he told her with a laugh. "Ideally, there would be a team of codebreakers working on the same material, trying every process at the same time until someone broke through. As it is just me, it is neither efficient nor effective." He rubbed at his eyes with a wry exhale. "Weaver wants us to find answers to questions we haven't asked yet so that we can stop being a step behind the Faction. I feel as though I need to write him with the unfortunate revelation that we are four steps behind at least."

"Why in the world would they send just two of us when an entire team is needed?" Hal muttered, shaking her head. "A fool's errand, if ever I've heard one. I can intercept every letter I can nick from Leclerc's pockets, but without the means to translate them, it isn't useful. And without that information, my drawing abilities don't help us at all." She managed a quick smile. "Unless we start tracking Leclerc like one of Gent's children. Note every person he associates with and every location he frequents. Infiltrate his household, perhaps."

John had to laugh at the idea, which also helped to relieve his present tension somewhat. "It is likely because it is a fool's errand that they only sent us. They can't spare the operatives and assets, and it's clear that if letters have been intercepted before, they haven't had success in deciphering them."

Hal grunted a noncommittal sound. "Which leaves us nowhere and with nothing to go on."

"Correct." He gave her a flat smile. "Any success on placing

Monsieur Fontaine with a mission?"

She shook her head, her frown deepening. "No. I can't risk sending out the drawing I've made with his name, no matter how secure Ruse might think the connections between here and England are. I've never wanted to know the details of missions and assignments before, but now…"

He let the silence hang between them rather than attempt an answer.

"Well," he finally said on an exhale, "should we go out? Attempt to find something else to occupy our minds or find other connections?"

Hal raised a brow at him. "We've been to gatherings almost every night since we've arrived in Paris, and you want to go out again? To what purpose? Our list of potential suspects goes beyond two pages because we have no means of paring it down."

"Why not just go out for ourselves?" John inquired in a tone much lower than he intended, hesitancy nearly choking him as soon as the words left his mouth.

He was not a social creature; Hal was not a social creature. Why would they intentionally be social without a purpose? A quiet evening at home was far more his style and his taste, and he suspected she was much the same.

Suddenly, he could picture the pair of them sitting in a quiet parlor far from their present one, a book in his hand and an easel before her. A fire flickered in the room, and its crackling accompanied a clock as the only sounds to be heard. Peaceful, comfortable, and natural. Such contentment in one image!

And Hal being there was the best of all contentment.

How could that be?

"I hadn't considered that," Hal murmured, bringing him back to the suggestion he'd had that he now wanted to take back. "What a relief it would be to be alone."

Or perhaps he'd been a genius after all.

"Indeed," he managed. "We could even go to the opera."

Now he was completely, entirely, and undoubtedly mad.

Hal must have thought the same by her present expression.

"The opera?" she laughed. "You have intentions to suffer this evening?"

He chuckled and shrugged a shoulder, rubbing one arm absently. "It keeps us from having to be particularly social while still actually attending a sociable event. Alone in a room filled with people we have no need to associate with."

A thudding from out in the corridor followed by peals of giggles made them both sigh, though with amusement more than irritation.

"The opera it is," Hal all but announced. "Rossini or the other one?"

"Whichever suits you, *Ange*," he said, waving off any responsibility of the decision. "I attend so seldom in London that almost anything will be new to me."

His wife grinned and nodded, rising from her chair. "We'll try the other, then. I've never even heard of it, and it may be interesting if Leclerc enjoys it so."

"It could also be a perfect opportunity to nap in public," John pointed out.

"Which would also be a pleasant use of our time," Hal shot back. Then she wrinkled up her nose. "I suppose it would be polite to at least extend the invitation to the others…"

John groaned but nodded all the same. "It would defeat the purpose, but politeness must be observed."

They shared a look that was so clearly in unison, it was a wonder they didn't express the feelings behind them more frankly.

What in the world could that mean?

As Hal left to offer the invitations, and no doubt to change for the evening, John stared at nothing in particular, his mind spinning on an entirely different puzzle altogether.

When had Hal ceased to be a trial and become his *Ange* in truth? When had he found comfort in her rather than conflict? Why did spending more time with her seem to be the best use of his time, and the desire to be alone with her more prominent than to be alone himself? How had he found himself so changed so quickly, and yet feel more like the truth of himself at the same time?

For the first time in many long years, he found himself wishing his brother were somewhere in the vicinity to confer with. Though Jeremy was a rogue and a rapscallion, his advice was usually sound.

And he would have a far better idea of these matters than John could ever hope to.

But Jeremy wasn't here, and he had nothing to go on but his instincts and his desires.

At the moment, they were aligned and told him to spend the evening at the opera with his wife.

His wife.

What a concept.

With that in mind, John took himself off to his rooms to let Leys make him into as much of a peacock as he might wish, not entirely caring what he looked like this evening so long as he was with Hal. Undoubtedly, she would look overdone as well, and the pair of them could laugh about it without the worry of behaving in a certain manner.

An hour later, which seemed a ridiculous amount of time for a man to be situated in apparel no matter what the occasion, John stepped back out into the adjoining parlor.

"*Ange*?" he called.

"One moment more," came the almost cheery response. "Collette needs to put on a finishing touch!"

John smiled to himself and began to pace the room aimlessly, the strange lightness in his heart feeling entirely foreign but not unpleasant.

Not at all unpleasant, actually.

He'd never felt anything like it, especially during an assignment. He should have been climbing the walls in agitation over his lack of progress in his work, but instead…

"All right, now I am ready."

He turned, thought unfinished, and instantly lost any ability to think at all.

What stood before him was a vision belonging on a canvas with meticulous paints attempting and failing to capture the brilliance, magnificence, and beauty in a transcendent, timeless manner. Not a living, breathing, perfectly mortal being sharing the same air he was.

The gown itself was lovely, a shade of blue pulled directly from the palest part of the sky, beaded and embroidered with white flowers and vines that created the illusion of an ethereal garden. The tiny sleeves hung precariously at her shoulders, the expanse of porcelain skin more arresting than the details of the gown itself. Flawless skin, bare from shoulder to shoulder, her neck free from any accessory that would have detracted from her perfection.

Simple, undeniable perfection.

The neckline was surprisingly modest considering the shoulder line, the hint of lace bordering it tempting any imagination to drift there, though John surpassed all that by returning his attention to her face.

Her cheeks held the faintest blush, her smile tucked in a shy expression of inner delight, either at his reaction or her own. And that smile would have undone any man with blood in his veins.

"*Ange*…" he breathed, unable to voice her name any louder, reverence of expression seeming poignantly accurate.

She lifted a trim brow at him. "*Merci beaucoup, monsieur.*"

"*Non, madame.*" He shook his head and closed the distance between them, lifting a gloved hand to his lips. "*C'est moi qui dois vous remercier. Merci mille fois.*"

He felt her breath catch as much as he heard it, and the desire to smile became irresistible.

"Shall we?" he inquired, his mouth barely lifting from the surface of her glove.

He watched Hal's throat work for a swallow. "I think we must," she whispered, her fingers fluttering in his hold.

He nodded and led her towards the door, hardly a word spoken between them as they ventured down to the entrance to retrieve their outerwear.

De Rouvroy met them there, all smiles. "I do hope you have a pleasant evening. Enjoy the opera. I am pleased someone will make use of the box other than René."

Hal smiled for her cousin as she was helped into her cloak. "Are you sure you won't accompany us?"

John gave her an exasperated look over her cousin's shoulder, making her giggle.

"I think not," de Rouvroy answered without concern. "It is not an opera I am fond of. I do not share my son's appreciation for every opera, I fear. But perhaps you will find it to your tastes."

"I do hope so." Hal smiled again and pulled her cloak around her further. "John?"

His knees were suddenly jolted with a sharp sensation, though he wouldn't call it unpleasant. Weak yet strong, numb yet filled with energy, frozen in place yet aching to move. All because of his name from her lips.

"Yes," he replied, not entirely sure what question he was answering, or if he gave the right response. Taking a risk, he extended his arm to her. He exhaled silently when she took it, then escorted her to the waiting coach.

They didn't exchange words on the short drive to the theatre, the air between them thick with unspoken tension. Silently John helped her from the coach, silently they entered the building, and silently they made their way to the box reserved regularly for members of the de Rouvroy family. John had always been comfortable with silence, never seeing the need to fill it unnecessarily, and the intensity of this silence was no different. There was a divinely comfortable feeling to it, though he had never felt a more uncomfortable comfort in his life.

The contradiction in such a thing was not lost on him.

"So many of our new friends are here," Hal murmured aloud as she sat and glanced about the theatre.

"Are they?" he asked, not wishing to look anywhere else.

She nodded, indicating with her head. "Leclerc, Savatiers, Marchands, Bouchers, Degarmo... The gentleman whose name I have never seen written so I can never remember…"

"Roussell," John reminded her. "And I don't particularly care, *Ange*."

Hal glanced at him then, her breathing seeming a trifle faster than normal. "No?"

He slowly shook his head. "As far as I'm concerned, I'm here alone. With you."

Her full lips quirked into a dazzling smile, and she returned her attention to the stage, the grand overture striking up.

John watched her for a long moment, torn between taking her hand and simply fiddling with her skirt like a child. The fabric was close enough to do so, and the hand just out of reach in her lap. Yet he had to be connected to her somehow, had to cross the barrier between them that taunted him so.

Smiling to himself, he pulled his glove off and laid it in his lap, then reached out two fingers to gently, almost absently, stroke the skin of her upper arm from just above her elbow to just beneath her precarious sleeve.

He watched her take in a sharp breath, never slowing or stilling in the deliberately grazing action, waiting for her to shift away. But his clever wife settled more fully into her seat, even shifted a hair closer to him, and continued to watch the stage.

A wave of bumps began to appear on the skin of her arm, her neck, her shoulders, and John found himself wearing a more satisfied, secret smile for the remainder of the opera. The friction of his fingers against her arm was the most delicious sensation he had ever known.

Chapter Ten

Hal walked silently beside John, arms folded tightly about her, his hand almost protectively at her back, each of them shaking their heads. It was madness to be meeting him so close to their current residence, and with their evening being so carefully scheduled? It would be fortunate indeed if Leys and Collette did not hang them both from their bedposts by the ankles in joint mutiny.

"Utterly ridiculous," Hal muttered under her breath. "I'll have you know I am already in my stays, and they chafe with the utmost discomfort to move at this speed."

"I could have gone my entire life without knowing that," John replied, his tone completely unconcerned and mild.

Hal bit back a snarl and opted not to jab her elbow into his side at the present, but only because it would slow their progress, and they had no time for that. "This had better be crucial to our evening."

"Oh, it is, Sketch."

She gasped and stumbled into John as Ruse stepped out from between buildings just to her left. "Bloody hellfire and brimstone…" she managed, though her heart was still pounding in her throat, John's hands protectively at her upper arms.

Ruse grinned in a manner completely unapologetic. "Not quite, but close." He tipped his cap at them both, choosing to linger in the shadowy interval between buildings. "Message from home."

Hal stepped closer to him, John just behind. "Yes?"

"There will be a fellow operative in attendance tonight," Ruse informed them, leaning against the wall rather like Hal had seen Gent do a time or two. "You won't know him by sight, and he will give no indication he recognizes or knows either of you."

"Then why tell us at all?" John inquired in the same steady voice he had used before. "Surely, the less we know…"

Ruse nodded once, very firmly. "You won't know. Not unless it is utterly necessary. But he will be of use if he sees an opportunity."

"Why haven't we met with him?" Hal asked, a shiver racing through her with the chill of the breeze. "If he knows something that could aid us, why keep us apart?"

"Truth be told, we were not entirely sure when he would be in Paris next." Ruse shrugged and nudged his cap up, rubbing a dirty thumb across his brow. "His assignment has been going on for years, and our contact with him is minimal at best. He was in London long enough to report, was told about your assignment, and is here just for tonight, just for this ball."

Hal looked at John in horror, apprehension weaving its way through her. She saw the same emotions reflected in his eyes. Slowly, they looked at Ruse again.

"Why?" John's question was slow and filled with a weight that had Hal inching closer to him.

Ruse exhaled once. "Because his contacts tell him that certain Faction members will be meeting tonight at the ball. I don't know who, and I don't know where," he insisted before they could ask the question.

Hal bit her lip to keep from asking it anyway.

"He only said he would feel himself best used to join in the evening with you, step in if he must, but observe if that was all that was required." Ruse readjusted his cap and looked between them both. "I don't know what else to tell you. But tonight could be important."

"Marvelous," Hal replied. "Is that all?"

Ruse grinned at her, then looked at John. "Is she always like that?"

"Yes," John grunted, the hand at Hal's back pressing more fully against her in a gesture of comfort. "This is her polite side."

Hal forced a cheeky smile for effect.

That made Ruse snort softly. "Right. Enjoy the evening. We'll be around if you need us." He nodded at them, then slipped away without another word.

Hal watched him go, then looked up at John. "What is the point of him? Honestly. We didn't need to know any of that, and we got no information out of anything he said."

John rolled his eyes heavenward and turned them both back the way they had come. "I haven't the faintest idea. We're not alone?"

"But we are," Hal pointed out. "This operative might not even make himself known to us."

"To let us know we have work to do tonight?" he offered.

"Because that makes this different from any other night we are out in company."

"Perhaps he simply wanted to see you."

Hal paused a step and gave him a derisive look. "Really?"

John chuckled and seemed to consider the idea. "I don't know, it's not such a foregone conclusion. You are quite unique, you know, and undeniably pretty."

"Stop that." She scowled through her blush, instinctively folding her arms once more.

"It's true," her husband insisted in a maddeningly calm voice. "A vision of beauty. Why wouldn't a man invent a reason to see you?"

Hal's cheeks would likely never return to their natural shade again. John wasn't normally so flattering or flirtatious, and she wouldn't have even called this charming were he any other man. But he wasn't any other man, and that made his words all the more difficult to hear.

Everything John ever said had a vein of truth, even when teasing.

She couldn't dwell on what significance that had, considering what had been said.

"Well," she grumbled as she averted her eyes, "he'd do well to remember that I'm a married woman and have neither the time nor the inclination to indulge his fancies."

"Too right," came the firm, almost relieved reply.

She wasn't about to interpret that either.

Hurrying back to the de Rouvroy home, they parted ways in the parlor to be trussed up for the evening, and barely had a look at each other before they were nearly racing down to the entrance hall to meet the others and load into carriages.

As the coach rambled on, Hal was fussing with her entire ensemble. "I just know I've forgotten something. Colette was literally stabbing my scalp with pearl pins as I was walking out to meet you."

"I think I'm slowly being strangled to death," John shot back, tugging at the tight space between his cravat and his neck. "And it's pinned. It's an emerald, isn't it?"

"Yes, and it's lovely." Hal scoffed softly and turned to him. "Here, just a moment." She carefully unpinned it and assisted him in loosening the linen just enough to give him some comfort while not disrupting Leys' intricate design. Fixing the pin again, she nodded and patted the linen, smoothing it down just a little. "There. Better?"

John heaved a deep exhale. "Much." He grinned and his eyes drifted up to her hair. "You've a pin that's sitting rather precariously. May I?"

She nodded quickly. "Please. These likely cost more than my dowry. I dare not lose one."

"My more pressing concern was that you would appear unbalanced in your accoutrements," he laughed, carefully working the pin in question out. "What judgment would come upon you!" He smoothed down a bit of her hair, then gingerly replaced the pin with more security into the folds of her hair. "And done."

"It's not too towering, is it?" Hal winced even as she asked the question. "I caught a glimpse, and it does seem rather perilous in its dimension."

John shook his head as his eyes traced over the entire coiffure. "Not at all, it suits you very well. Elegant and refined, and perhaps more than one might see in a London ballroom, but no one will stare in awe or amazement. At your hair, at any rate." He winked, his smile turning crooked.

Hal slapped his chest playfully. "Wretch."

"It was a compliment!" he protested. "You look beautiful, *Ange*."

She ignored the twinge of delight that spread heat into her fingertips. "And you look both handsome and smart," she informed him with a sniff. "Only a little bit peacock, so you will go practically unnoticed among the over-trimmed and over-inflated."

"Thank you." He sat back and sighed, closing his eyes and seeming truly fatigued for the first time that day. "What I wouldn't give to claim to feel unwell tonight, *Ange*, and spend the quiet evening at home with you."

She'd have matched his pose had her restrictive stays and coiled hair not prevented her. "Did you forget the children are at the house? Surely, not so quiet."

He made a face of indifference. "They'd have gone to bed soon enough. And one doesn't have to pretend with children, so perhaps that would be preferable."

"Perhaps." She watched him for a long moment, wondering if he might truly sleep on the drive over. Then she felt her lips curve in an impish manner. "Will you dance with me tonight?"

He opened his eyes and rolled his head along the carriage seat to look at her. "Don't I always?"

Hal laughed once. "We've only been to small gatherings with small dances since we've been in Paris. This is our first grand affair, and I want to know if I might expect a dance with my husband."

He smiled at her, the sort of smile that curled the edges of her stomach into coils and set off explosions in the tips of each toe. "You may expect at least two, *Ange*. If I can get to you through the admiring throng."

"Just charge in," she suggested, returning his smile with all the warmth she currently felt. "Push them aside. Carry me off in front of the lot and claim me for all to see."

John quirked his brows in an almost suggestive manner. "Rather savage of me, wouldn't you say? Almost uncouth, certainly unrefined."

"Oh, I don't think so," Hal murmured, reaching out to unnecessarily adjust a bit of hair at his temple. "Perhaps just a little untamed, but I shouldn't mind that every now and again."

"No?"

She shook her head. "A girl likes to see a glimpse of the rugged hero within."

His eyes turned a shade more serious. "I'm a scholar, Hal."

"All the more reason to do so. The effect will be all the greater for the shock of it." She continued to smile, her fingers still moving over and over that hair at his temple, her husband going almost completely still at her touch. "Just come to me," she pleaded in a lower tone. "Wherever I am, however you ask, I'll come."

"Why do you sound afraid?" John asked, matching her volume and her mood. He reached up and brushed a thumb along her cheek, and she followed the touch, almost nuzzling into it. "What is it?"

Hal inhaled a shuddering breath, her hand falling to John's shoulder.

"I don't know," she whispered. "Everything. Anything. Suddenly, all I am is afraid."

"Don't be." John sat up and cupped her face in both hands, his eyes steady on hers. "*Ange*, don't be. We're here together, remember? Partners, not only spouses. There may be danger, yes, but we've got protection. Ruse and his fellows, this new operative… And we have each other."

"That's what I'm afraid of," she admitted before she could stop herself.

A deep furrow appeared between John's brows. "What do you…?"

His words faded as the carriage stopped, signaling their arrival at the ball.

The pause was just long enough for Hal to recollect her senses and shake herself free from the breathless respite her husband's hands provided.

"Right," she said brusquely, tugging at her gloves. "Armor in place, weapons ready?"

"I hope you don't mean my pin," he replied in an almost convincingly light tone, blessedly allowing the previous conversation to die. "If that's all I've got, we're doomed."

Hal pretended to be put out by that. "Why is it always down to the women to do the saving?" she asked aloud.

John stepped out of the carriage, nodding at the footman, then gave her a look as he extended a hand. "Because the men are hopeless without the women."

Hal's mouth popped open, then she tilted her head and gave her husband a rather smug smile as she took his hand. "I always knew you were a brilliant man."

"Glad to hear it," he grunted, tugging her cloak around the front of one shoulder. "I've been waiting for you to say that for *years*."

There was nothing to say or do but roll her eyes and lamely take the arm of the impertinent man beside her, letting him lead them both into the home of their host for the evening, Baron Voclain. Apparently, he was a close friend of the de Rouvroy family, had wealth to match theirs, and had the same appreciation for finery.

One could only hope that he had more restraint than her relations in the decor of his home.

But then, this was the social elite of Paris. Nothing was certain.

Their usual procession moved as one into the house, Agathe and René bickering as they usually did, which seemed ridiculous as René was a grown man and Agathe nearly an adult woman, but siblings know no maturity with each other. A line of footmen waited within to take cloaks, capes, and wraps from arriving guests, and Hal found herself touching the back of her hair to check its security.

"You look *si belle*," Agathe told her quickly, smiling in a way Hal had never seen. "I'm quite envious."

"Are you really?" Hal looked down at her cream gown, embroidered across the bodice and hemline with elegant rosettes in pale pink. She glanced up at Agathe sheepishly. "I forgot entirely what I was wearing, so in haste was I to prepare."

Agathe giggled and took her hand, squeezing. "One would never know."

Hal smiled back, marveling at the change such a smile wrought upon the young woman's already lovely features. "Well, I cannot compare to you this evening, *cousine*. You will have a suitor for every day of the week once the night is out."

"One worthy suitor would do," Agathe confessed with a dark glare towards her brother, who was too busy greeting their hostess to notice.

Was René somehow preventing his sister from finding a suitor? Intervening between Agathe and a particular would-be suitor? Hal opened her mouth to ask when their group moved on.

"What in the name of heaven was that?" John murmured, eyeing Agathe ahead of them.

"I haven't the faintest idea." Hal shook her head, a curious smile crossing her lips. "I think perhaps Agathe is not the spoiled chit I took her for, and she is only unhappy."

John made a noncommittal sound of acknowledgment. "Fancy that. She's right, you know."

Hal glanced up at him, frowning. "About what?"

His eyes darkened, his lips barely curving into a hint of a smile. "*Si belle, Ange.*"

She blinked at the rough, low words, and a stuttering exhale made its way from her.

"I can't think," she admitted in a raw tone.

His hint of a smile deepened.

"Welcome to the last two weeks of my life, *Ange*. And it's only getting worse the more time I spend with you."

Good heavens, she would burst into flames on the spot. Just incinerate in the center of the guests like some pagan bonfire for them to dance around. It would be a most memorable end, but an end all the same.

"I must claim the first dance, *Cousine* Henrietta," Jean exclaimed as they entered the ballroom, the strains of music already in full force.

Hal stared at him wide-eyed, still feeling rather singed in places. "Oh, but…"

"Go," John urged gently. "I'll find you later. I'll partner Agathe, if she'll have me."

One glance at Agathe told them both the heavens had just opened, and she nodded with such enthusiasm the entire family laughed, René aside.

"Very well," Hal conceded, smiling for all. "Onward, Cousin Jean."

He bowed grandly, winked at his wife, and whisked Hal to the center of the ballroom. She glanced over her shoulder briefly for just a glimpse of John, catching a secret, proud smile that she would have danced all night for.

A warm tingle raced down her spine, and she grinned in anticipation of the dance with him to come.

He'd put it off for as long as he could, and now he was two hairs short of madness.

He needed to find Hal, and he needed to dance with her.

Now.

And he had never felt such a drive and desperation to do anything so lively as dance in his entire life.

At the moment, John couldn't be entirely sure where she was. They'd been near each other several times over the course of the night, but he could honestly say he hadn't spent more than a few minutes in her company. Hadn't exchanged more than a handful of words with her. Hadn't touched her since they'd parted for the first dance.

He felt shockingly bereft as a result.

Logically, none of this made any sense to him, but somehow, he knew that dancing with his wife would set him to rights.

His wife.

How did such a simple description make him smile so easily? Hal had been his wife for some time now, for the entirety of this mission, and yet…

Yet…

Something had changed of late, and everything between them felt new, exciting, and important.

Painfully so, if pain could be a pleasant thing.

It made absolutely no sense. They had both been mingling with the other guests, prodding carefully for any information that might help them discover what might transpire that night. He'd been more congenial than he had ever managed in his life, laughed without any genuine amusement, and pretended to have interest in the most ludicrous things, all for the sake of their assignment. And his thoughts somehow still turned to the person of his wife?

Unfathomable, under the pressures of the night.

He scanned the guests around him, smiling at the few who had greeted him at some point in the evening. Then, he felt warmth envelop his body when he caught sight of Hal, looking angelic as usual, in conversation with Madame Savatier. Though each of the women would be considered lovely in appearance by their own rights, there could be no comparison in John's eyes.

Far and away, Hal was the fairer of the two, the one who would draw all eyes upon her, the one who could have lit the room simply by smiling, the one whom any man in the room should have coveted and any woman envied.

His feet were moving before he knew they had done so, and he had reached her before he'd found the words to speak.

Hal smiled at him, the sweet curve of her lips seeming to know exactly what torment he felt. "You've come to me," she murmured, her fair eyes dancing.

"Yes," he rasped in response, finding no more polite way to express himself. He extended a hand to her, a sudden fear of rejection striking him with agonizing depth.

The sensation of her hand being placed in his was heaven on earth, and the fact that he had strength in his legs to walk with her was nothing short of miraculous.

"At last," Hal said on a sigh.

Words and thoughts spun in John's mind, and he chanced a glance at her. "Have you been waiting to dance?"

Surely, she couldn't… Surely, she didn't…

She grinned rather slyly and quirked a brow. "Yes and no. I've wanted to dance with you all night, but I was desperate to break from conversation with Madame Savatier. She's a dear woman, but why in the world does anyone care about pickups at the hemline and whether they will become the popular fashion?"

John laughed at her exasperated expression, louder and harder than he would ever have done in public before, but unable to do anything less. Sometimes he just loved Hal, and her surprisingly direct, unusual view of life. Sometimes he just loved her sense of humor.

Sometimes he just loved her.

He loved her.

Laughter began to fade, but the warmth of it only grew, centering itself somewhere between his heart and his stomach. It expanded as he looked upon her from the line in which he stood, swirled about as she smiled at his amusement, spun itself around his head as he bowed towards her. The moment his hand touched hers in the dance, another wave of the sensation enveloped him, streaking its way into every vein in his body, every fiber of his being.

He was in love with Hal.

And he couldn't take his eyes off her.

He watched as she circled the man to his left, catching every change in her smile, every movement of her eyes, which flicked towards him more than once. When it was his turn, he circled the woman to her right, giving all due deference to his present partner, as was polite, but always looking back to Hal, anticipation building. The color in Hal's cheeks began to grow, adding to the rosy hue that seemed to pervade her from the moment she walked into the building this evening.

They met in the center, taking each other's hands, and there seemed to be a joint catching of breath, though nothing audible was emitted. Slowly, in time with the music and the other couple, they began to promenade, eyes solely on each other.

How could a heartbeat change so much as to march in exact time with the music about them? John could honestly say he was no skilled dancer, but he'd never needed to keep count in his head to be sure of his steps. Yet the cadence of his pulse allowed him to keep his focus where he wished it and not where the dance required him to.

They parted for the dance movement, took the hands of the dancers on either side of them and progressed backwards a slow three steps, each one seeming painful as they took him away from her.

The lead couple progressed down the line, and John felt his fingers buzzing by his sides, the waiting agonizing. Couple after couple followed, and at long last it was their turn, again taking hands and proceeding down the line. Hal wasn't smiling now, not exactly, but there was a slight curve to her lips that made him wild to kiss them.

Kiss Hal? In the middle of this ballroom in Paris?

It didn't seem like such a bad idea, which was clearly an indication of the madness of love if he'd ever heard one.

His eyes rose to hers, and the shade of blue there was darker than he recalled from only moments before. It nearly undid him.

The movement of the dance parted them once more, a groan seeming to rise from his entire frame at doing so. He circled around with the other men to move the line back to the front of the ballroom, staring at Hal without any shame or hesitation. She bit down on her lip just a bit, the gesture surely a sign of inner conflict or nerves, but it attracted him enough that his stomach clenched at the sight.

One more motion before the cycle started again… The partners met in the center of the line, standing close, hands pressing together, palm to palm, and turned slowly towards the right.

It might as well have been happening twice as slow as reality for him. He knew every breath she took, could have countered it with one of his own, felt her pulse as much as he felt his own, and the room faded from all existence but for the two of them. There were no other dancers, no guests, no hosts, and no mission.

There was only Hal.

Only his *Ange*.

The name for her had never before seemed so entirely apt.

"*Ange*," he breathed as their hands began to peel away from each other, his fingers running the length of her gloved forearm before parting completely.

Her lashes fluttered briefly, one breath exhaling in a rough near gasp that weakened his knees.

Then they were backing up into their lines once more, the distance between them suddenly an insurmountable obstacle that caused him physical pain.

Did it do the same for her?

He'd never been a praying man, but suddenly, the most devout petitions were sent to the heavens that she would feel as he did. That she could feel so.

That he was not alone.

A sound behind the line of ladies shook his concentration just long enough to wrench his attention from his wife to some motion behind her. There was nothing he could see that should have disturbed the dance at all, and yet his eyes shifted along the line of guests to discover Leclerc meandering his way through the group. Not unusual, Leclerc was a bit of a social puppy.

But then, as he moved to again turn with the lady on Hal's right, he saw Fontaine heading in the same direction. As well as Savatier, their host Voclain, and two other gentlemen, none of them acknowledging the other or seeming to have any coordination to the exodus at all.

Yet why would a host ever leave the ballroom?

John frowned as he approached Hal for the dance. "Something's happening," he murmured.

"I know," she replied, her attention behind the men. Then she looked up at him. "We have to follow."

As much as he hated to admit it, that had been his conclusion, as well. The dance had to end so their mission could continue.

He nodded, fighting back a resigned sigh. "I'll follow your lead."

Hal exhaled shortly, a crease appearing in her brow, then she stumbled just a little, swaying into him. "Oh…"

John swept her out of the dance at once, both of their feet moving quickly. "Come along, dear, let's find you some air."

"Air," she wheezed, a fairly passable impression of weakness taking over her. "Please…"

Madame Voclain was to them in a moment. "My dear, what is it?"

"Just a bit overcome," John assured her with a smile. "The excitement and splendor along with such lively dancing, it's quite done her in. Might there be a small parlor or some such where I might take her to recover herself?"

"*Oui*, just out of the doors and to the right." She looked at Hal pityingly. "Oh, my dear. Let me come with you, let me help you."

Hal shook her head, lolling it against John. "No, madame, please. Your guests… I'll be well presently…"

"I will tend to her, madame," John assured her. "Please, see to your guests. We insist."

The woman did not look convinced but nodded all the same and gestured toward the ballroom door.

John inclined his head in thanks and moved Hal as quickly as a husband might have moved a swooning wife out of the public eye. "Nicely done, *Ange*," he told her, fighting a smile.

"I've been preparing my entire life for this act," she retorted as one of her hands clutched at his coat. They exited the ballroom and turned to the right, as directed, at which time Hal was recovered and giving John a firm look. "Let's find ourselves a meeting, shall we?"

Chapter Eleven

"They wouldn't be that obvious, would they?"

"Sometimes the obvious is the least expected."

"But the card room?" Hal shook her head, exhaling in a strange sort of disappointment. "They cannot control all of the men in there."

John gave her an exasperated look. "They'll be controlling us in a moment if you don't lower your voice."

Hal made a face and stuck her tongue out. Then she began eyeing the corridor carefully. "How to hear without being seen? How to…?" She suddenly grinned and nodded to herself before glancing up at John. "Sometimes I adore large houses with lots of servants."

His brow creased in confusion. "Why?"

For a brilliant man, he could be rather thick at times.

"Honestly, John," she groaned in a whisper. "Didn't you ever sneak about in the servants' corridors? Their nooks and crannies that aren't visible to the naked eye?"

"No," he replied with the clearest, most innocent expression known to man. "Jeremy did, though."

That was not surprising in the least. Hal sighed and extended a hand to him.

"Then you are long overdue."

He took her hand with a quizzical smile, the pressure of his firm grip making her smile almost dreamily as she had in the dance they'd shared.

Well, started to share.

She scowled mentally at the recollection, and turned, tugging her husband behind her as she pushed open a servant's door and headed down the dark, narrow corridor.

The only light available at present came from the faint outline of another doorway, and Hal moved there leaning against the wall alongside, John joining her.

Conversations in rapid French could be heard, the voices were low but not inaudible.

"*It's unrealistic to expect more from that quarter,*" a voice said, his French not quite native sounding. "*Until we get more pieces in place, we must wait.*"

"*What about Castleton?*" another, much lower voice asked.

"*His plan was idiotic and selfish,*" the first voice answered. "*There will be no assistance for him. British justice can have their way with him. He is of no use to us now.*"

A murmur of voices reacted to that, though no clear answers.

"*What about our key?*" a new voice asked. "*Has our hand received what is needed there?*"

Hal looked at John in confusion. "Key?" she breathed. "Hand?"

"Codes?" His voice was softer than a whisper, and she could hear his head shake.

"*Our key was no longer secure. They have been removed from their post for the sake of the cause and will soon find themselves at work in another way.*"

"*How?*"

"*If you needed to know, you would.*"

"*Sorry for my tardiness,*" a new voice interjected. "*J'ai vecu.*"

"*Vous ne me verrez pas mourir,*" the room replied in a strange unison.

What in the world was this? Hal had never heard the familiar Faction phrase used as a greeting and come with a response. Where had that come from?

"You shall not see me die," John recited in the same barely audible voice as before.

"I know what they said," Hal hissed as her mind spun on it. "I do know French, thank you."

John breathed a laugh. "I was simply reciting."

"Well, don't!" Hal tried to relax against the wall, her head leaning back against it.

"*What news from Calais?*" inquired someone. "*Are we ready for the next wave?*"

Hal shook her head. They were never going to get anywhere just listening; they would likely only know what was already known.

They needed something new.

"We have to find out who is in there."

"How?" John shifted closer, the side of his body nearly flush with hers. "We can't wait outside the room for them to come out."

Hal shook her head, the motion brushing her face along his shoulder. "No, and we can't distinguish voices." She exhaled and laid her head against him. "I have to go in there."

"What?" John hissed, his voice nearly too loud for their secrecy. "No!"

Hal shifted to face him, reaching up to cover his mouth, her eyes on his, barely discernible in the dark, but there all the same. "Yes, John!"

He shook his head emphatically beneath her palm.

She gripped his coat in one hand, arching closer. "Yes! I have an excellent memory, it is true, but only if I *see* things! I have to see them, John, so I can draw them."

His hands flew to her upper arms, his grip tight. Beneath her palm, his mouth was still, and he didn't struggle, which she took as a surrender of sorts. She slid her hand to his jaw, wishing there was more light, just enough to see him better.

"*Ange*..." John pressed his lips to her brow, lingering and resting his mouth at her hairline, breathing unsteadily against her skin. "I can't..."

Hal stroked his jaw softly, her eyes fluttering shut. "I have to. You have your gifts, and I have mine. I need this to be of use. You know that."

"I know," he whispered, his lips pressing against her in a warm, lingering kiss. "Doesn't mean I have to like it."

She smiled at that and nuzzled close, inhaling his scent. "Well, no. And I have no doubt they'll send me away quickly."

"I hope they do." John sighed and broke from her skin. He cupped her cheek with one hand and gently rubbed his thumb there.

"Be careful."

She nodded in his hold, turning her face and kissing the palm quickly. "You, too." She smiled, hoping he could feel it in his palm, then stepped aside and strode by him, desperately trying to ignore the last lingering feeling of his fingers on her arm.

Exhaling, she exited the corridor, squaring her shoulders. She would only have a moment or two, and she would need to make it count.

She fixed a polite smile on her face and pushed through the ajar door to the card room.

All conversation stopped, and all eyes fell on her.

Perfect.

Twelve men sat between three card tables, all grouped closely together, cards in hand, though it was not clear if anyone was actually playing. Had she not been listening a moment ago, she would never have known treason was occurring. Indeed, had she not seen Leclerc among the group, knowing the letters he carried, she might have doubted that these were the men whose conversations she'd heard.

"Oh my," she gasped in bright English, looking at each man in turn, though taking care not to linger long enough for concern. "I was looking for my husband. He accompanied me to the parlor when I needed to recover myself, then he abandoned me there. When he did not return, I feared he might have chosen cards over his wife."

Voclain rose, chuckling with what appeared to be good nature. "Alas, madame, we have not seen him, but I will be sure to scold him soundly for his neglect when he next appears."

Hal beamed and curtseyed. "Many thanks, monsieur. I am quite delighted, as it happens. My husband is dreadful at cards, and the lot of you would wind up pocketing his fortune."

A round of relatively stiff laughter sounded.

Voclain maintained his smile, though the strain was showing now. "Jacque, if you wouldn't mind showing Madame Pratt her way back to the ballroom? She will be missed by our guests." He nodded at Hal in a clear sign of dismissal. "We will send your husband to you the moment we see him."

"I thank you." She curtseyed again and glanced up at the very tall, very burly footman in livery that did not suit his stature.

It would appear she was leaving now.

"*Madame*," he grunted, blocking her progression any further into the room and gesturing for the door behind them.

Hal dipped her chin and turned, moving back into the corridor. "I am quite sure I know the way," she assured the footman that was clearly not a footman.

He shook his head. "I will see you back," he replied, his accent so thick the words were barely intelligible.

Well, there went reuniting with John, for the moment. How attentive would Jacque be with her once she was returned? What if she was not able to leave the ballroom again? How would she explain John's absence? Would they raise any suspicions?

All too soon, they had arrived at the ballroom, and she was very nearly shoved inside.

"*Merci,*" she mumbled, though the footman had already turned away.

Not too observant, it seems.

But then Jacque stood against the wall nearby, and Hal rolled her eyes to herself. "Now what?"

"Now, Madame Pratt," a new voice uttered just beside her, "we will take you back to the parlor so you will be seen to be recovering. Move. Now."

Firm hands settled in polite positions on her arms, though the grip was too tight for politeness. Hal swallowed a gasp and moved with the man out of the ballroom, the scent of aged spirits and cigar wafting through her nostrils. Yet he was no slovenly drunkard; on the contrary, he was clean-shaven and crisply dressed.

And his English was impeccable.

"Why?" Hal asked, not bothering to pretend politeness, though she did pretend at swooning airs once more.

"Because you were seen," came his cutting voice. "The pair of you were seen entering the servants' corridor. Certain attendees are now seeking those individuals, and we must establish that it was not you who was seen. Hurry. They're coming."

Hal's eyes widened, and her throat dried. She immediately strained towards the corridor, though her captor would not let her move much at all.

"Steady," the man soothed, surprisingly well. "He's safe. Come with me for just a moment, and we'll away soon."

Dozens of scenarios flashed through her mind, none particularly comfortable, and her parched throat ached. "What are you going to do with me?"

He snorted softly. "No need to fear me, Sketch. I do believe you were notified I may attend?"

Hal's eyes widened, and she nodded once. "Yes."

"Excellent. Then relax, but hurry, and go along with me."

She did so, letting him half carry her to the parlor, ignoring his jabbered explanation to any inquiring minds about her state and barked orders to find her husband.

The parlor was soon there, and Hal was deposited in a chair by a window. She immediately put a hand to her brow and set her fan to work, her pulse racing with the anxieties of her plight.

Footsteps hurried along the corridor, paused, then continued on without entering.

She exhaled roughly with overwhelming relief.

"Don't relax yet," her companion hissed.

More footsteps thundered nearby.

"*Ma chère cousine*," Jean blustered, barging into the room and falling to his knees beside her. "Are you well? What is wrong?"

Hal bit back a curse and gave her cousin a tired smile. "Nothing, cousin. A trifle weak, a little dizzy. I became quite overcome, but I shall be well presently."

Jean didn't seem convinced and looked around the room. "Where is your husband?" he demanded. "He should be here!"

"Signore Pratt has gone to fetch the coach for the signora," her ally informed her cousin in a pristine Italian accent. "I offered to mind her until all was in readiness."

Jean's almost reverent intake of breath was comical. "Signore Romano… you have our sincere thanks. Such gracious care, monsieur."

"It is nothing," Romano replied, raising a protesting hand. "Please, return to the party. She is well looked after."

Jean looked back at Hal with a smile, a knowing light entering his eyes. "If you are unwell from dancing, Henrietta, perhaps you may have something to announce soon…?"

Hal blushed instantly, realizing to what he referred, and he took her blushes for another reason entirely.

"I shall await such blessed tidings." He leaned in to kiss her cheek and left the parlor, clasping his son on the shoulder as he lingered just outside.

Once their steps had faded, Hal dropped her hand, shaking her head. "That was mortifying."

Romano laughed once. "Only because they are real relations who may actually want to hear such things. Perhaps Sphinx can be persuaded?"

Hal glared at him despite the sudden burst of warmth hitting her stomach at the suggestion.

Romano's chuckles continued, and he nodded. "Fair enough. Let us away now before questions are asked."

She rose with a sigh and looked up at him. "Won't more questions be asked because we are leaving?"

"Shouldn't be," he grunted. "We have witnesses that you left the dance in distress, were seen recovering in the parlor, and later were seen leaving with assistance."

"And my husband?" Her voice hitched in distress, hating that she hadn't seen him, didn't know where he was, how he was, or if he knew…

Romano sighed. "I don't know, pet. I can only trust Ruse to make it convincing."

"Don't call me pet," Hal snarled as they neared the foyer. "It's so patronizing."

Servants sprang forward once they neared the front, eager to serve.

"Monsieur Pratt," Romano announced her husband's name to the nearest servant in perfect English. "I ordered my carriage readied?"

"*Oui, Monsieur Pratt,*" a footman confirmed with a sharp bow and click of heels. He gestured the way while other servants grabbed their outerwear.

"How did you…?" Hal hissed, letting the question hang.

Romano made a show of assisting her with her cloak. "I look

enough like your husband to pass for him when someone doesn't know better." He smiled quickly, dark eyes sparkling. "Servants relegated to the entrance at these things never know better."

Hal smirked at him as he offered an arm and led her out. "Taking quite a chance."

"Odds are with us." He shrugged and loaded her into the carriage, following quickly.

The carriage pulled away at once, and Hal breathed a sigh of relief. "Thank you."

"Not at all," he replied easily. "Did you get what you needed?"

She nodded, staring at him with some fascination. "I think so." She shook her head. "I know you somehow. I remember your face."

He grinned slowly. "You should. I was at your parents' home often enough when you were naught but a chick."

A hint of Irish brogue started to seep into his voice, and Hal knew at once this was his natural accent. It fit her blurry memories and felt right within them.

"Were you?" Hal bit her lip, brow furrowing in thought. "But… my father…"

"A good mate," he told her, nodding. "A good operative. Most of my meetings, however, were with your mother."

Hal stilled, the rocking of the coach doing nothing to shift her one way or the other. "Mama?"

Again, he nodded. "I may be the only one who can tell you this, Sketch, but she was the best damned operative I have ever known, especially considering she was never at the Convent."

"I knew she was skilled." Hal swallowed with some difficulty, choosing her words with care. "But… for whom? That was never made clear, and considering the events of her death…"

"She was for England, Sketch." Romano reached out for her hand and squeezed gently. "She loved France, would always love France, which was why she was willing to risk so much to aid the country of her birth. But her loyalty was to us. She was the only one at the time who could successfully infiltrate both sides, and she did so flawlessly. Up until the end."

Hal's eyes swam in tears. "How can you be sure?"

She received an almost fatherly smile in return. "Because I took over for her in the aftermath. My role now is the one she created. I know everything she knew, every contact she made, every missive she wrote. England owes her a great debt, and we can never repay."

"I always wondered…" Hal murmured. "I hoped…"

"You're very much like her, you know. Coloring aside." He tilted his head just a touch. "Her eyes were exactly the same shape. Your father used to call the pair of you the eyes of March." He rolled his eyes at the horrible joke and shook his head in memory.

The same shaped eyes? But dark, like her cousin had said… Hal thought back to the sketch she had started in London of her mother, the one she could never get right, and instantly she itched to look at the eyes she had drawn. Now she'd have a far better reference for them, and perhaps that would get her even closer to accuracy.

"Your brother is your father, though," Romano said on an exhale, folding his arms. "Maddening, really, to be so uncanny a likeness and temperament."

"You know Trick?" Hal asked with a small smile.

He grunted once. "Too well, I'm afraid. I already prefer you to him."

"Excellent choice." Hal looked out of the window and frowned to herself. "We should be home by now."

"I asked for a longer route." Romano shrugged once. "Habit, I'm afraid. Never take the same route twice. It's sure to throw off scant pursuers."

Hal eyed him again, marveling at the habitual cleverness there. "Your accent leads me to suppose that your surname isn't actually Romano, sir, and that you are no Italian."

He only shrugged again. "Suppose away." He examined their surroundings and narrowed his eyes. "I'll take you to the door of the house, but not join you. De Rouvroy's servants are likely more observant than the ones we left. If anyone asks, tell them your husband wished to walk a while. People do so in Paris. Hopefully, he'll be along before too long. Ruse is good, I wouldn't worry."

"And what about you?" Hal asked, more curious than ever. "What will you do?"

"Continue on," he said evasively. "I'm always on the move, plenty to do, plenty to see. And plenty of people who are most anxious to see me."

Hal could only shake her head. "Why? What do they want?" she demanded. "Who are you?"

His smile deepened just a touch. "Only one question gets answered tonight, my dear Sketch. The name is Skean." He inclined his head in a sort of bow. "At your service."

Chapter Twelve

John slipped into the front door of the de Rouvroy home, his heart pounding, his mind swimming, his feet aching in odd places.

Darting about the streets of Paris after an evening of dancing was not an activity he would recommend to anyone, nor one he would be taking up again any time soon.

"*Avez-vous apprécié votre promenade, Monsieur Pratt?*" the butler asked as he approached, his smile more welcoming than anything John had expected after the night he'd had thus far.

John stared as he shrugged out of the overcoat Ruse had provided him and handed it over. How in the world had the man known John had been walking about Paris?

Our friend will have made up some story for Sketch. Whatever it is, go along.

Ruse's words to him only moments before echoed in John's mind, and he nodded, praying his hesitation and delay had not been as apparent to the man as it had felt. "Yes, thank you. Not so chilly this evening as it has been."

The butler nodded. "It will turn soon, I zink. Winter, you know."

Yes, John did know.

It rather felt like winter now, with various parts of him feeling particularly chilled, and the whole of him feeling especially exhausted.

"I shall retire now," John informed him, moving towards the stairs, wondering if he really was as terrible an actor as he felt.

But the butler seemed to notice nothing and only bowed. "*Oui, monsieur. Bonne nuit.*"

Good night, indeed. He wished it was a good night. He'd thought it might be a good night, and it had certainly appeared as though it might have been a good night while he was in it, but then...

How had everything shifted sideways *after* Hal had entered the card room? From what he could tell, she hadn't been forced out, and the conversation after she had left hadn't even remotely mentioned her as suspicious.

But then Ruse had appeared and shoved John further into the servants' corridor, down at least three more dark and cramped ones, then out into the Paris night. He'd explained as much as he could, that John and Hal had been spotted entering the corridor itself, and that, while their identities were safe, the danger was quite real. Thundering footsteps not far behind them had emphasized that fact, and it was only due to Ruse's keen knowledge of Paris that they had avoided being caught.

His brother Jeremy had often spoken of the adrenaline he'd felt on missions, particularly dangerous ones, and how alive it made him feel.

John felt vulnerable.

Alive, yes, but vulnerable.

It wasn't something he looked forward to feeling again. There was a reason he was more of an asset than an operative, and he looked forward to returning to that role.

Pushing into his bedchamber, nearly staggering with the fatigue that was catching up to him, he fumbled with the cravat around his neck, somehow still maintaining its ridiculous shape and style after all he'd been through. Yet it also came loose with remarkable ease once he removed the pin.

A flash of memory from earlier in the evening appeared before him, seeming to be days ago rather than hours. Hal smiling at the knotted linen, her deft fingers plucking out the pin and assisting him with its adjustment so that the evening might be more comfortable for his neck. She'd placed it back, and somehow the heat of her hands had seeped through the fabric straight to John's throat, leaving it parched and aching for relief.

She was afraid, she had said, but she hadn't given a reason. Hadn't confided that far, though the admission of fear seemed monumental.

She hadn't seemed afraid in their dance; on the contrary, she'd been more alive than he'd ever seen or felt, more real and tangible than anything he could bear witness to.

She hadn't been afraid in the darkness listening to the Faction members; she had been the one consoling *him*, though he had felt the slightest tremble in her frame as he'd held her close, as his lips had been at her skin.

John shuddered now and sank onto his bed. Where was Hal? Was she safe and whole? Had she escaped without detection, as he had?

Was she even now afraid?

He squeezed his eyes shut, averting his gaze in shame, though there was nothing in this room to bring him pain. He should have gone back for her; he should have argued more with Ruse to bring Hal with them. He should never have left her retrieval to someone else, especially someone he did not know and therefore could not trust. She was John's wife, for pity's sake. He had taken an oath to honor and protect her, and how had he done that tonight?

Had he vowed to love her as well? The memory of their unconventional wedding ceremony was hazy at best, considering its circumstances and his attitude surrounding it. He had no way to be sure if Weaver and Tailor had kept to the proper tradition of Anglican marriage ceremonies, or if they had adapted the service to be a more businesslike and legal transaction.

He hadn't loved her then, but he certainly loved her now, and he wouldn't sleep until he knew she was safe.

He pushed himself up from the bed and began to pace, agitation coursing over and through him in waves until he seemed to be drowning in it. Struggling for breath though there were no words to assign to the thoughts causing such sensations.

Ange.

Her name repeated over and over in his mind, a cadence to his body and mind that, for the moment, was his only anthem and prayer.

All he could consider.

Somehow, a sound broke through the frenzy of his thoughts, made him pause a step, his frame frozen as every hair stood on end, straining to hear it again.

He didn't dare breathe, didn't dare blink.

Then he heard it, something beyond his room, and, if possible, beyond the parlor, too.

The unmistakable sound of a hinge squeaking.

John moved with more speed than he would have thought possible if he'd been thinking. He wrenched open the connecting door to the parlor and stared at the closed door opposite him. He braced his arms on the doorframe, waiting, hoping…

A moment later, it opened, and there stood the blessed form of his wife. Well and whole, still in her ballgown, her hair half loosed, eyes wide, and gaping at him. She was completely and utterly perfect.

Somehow, a weak laugh escaped from the center of John's chest, and Hal shuddered a gasp, the sound carrying across the distance with startling ease.

Then they were moving, eyes locked on each other, their pace increasing with each step.

A broken sob passed Hal's lips as she leapt at him, and John caught her up in his arms, clutching her to him without shame.

"Oh, John," Hal gasped, her arms folding tightly about his neck. "Oh, heavens, you're safe."

John could only shake his head against her, burying his face into her hair as his frame shook with relief and fear. "*Ange*," he eventually managed. "My *Ange*…"

"I'm sorry." Hal hiccupped and pressed him closer. "I'm so sorry, John. I should never have gone in there… I shouldn't have risked… I shouldn't…"

"Hush," he murmured, sliding his lips to her ear, his arms encircling her back. "Nothing to be sorry for. This wasn't your fault, darling. Couldn't be."

Another cry broke from her, and John could nearly feel an accompanying crumple in her body. "John… Forgive me…"

Swallowing hard, he lifted his head from her and brought his hands to her face, letting her slide until her feet touched the floor and pulling her slightly away from him. He cupped her cheeks, his thumbs smoothing the steady stream of tears away. "*Ange*… look at me."

She opened her tear-splattered lashes, and the brightness of their shade almost startling in its beauty.

John brushed his thumb against her cheek again. "There is nothing to forgive. There is no blame to assign. You were magnificent, and brave beyond imagining. You risked everything for our assignment, as we should. As I should. But you… brilliant, breathtaking, beautiful you…" He shook his head, breaking off as his emotions surged. He leaned forward and pressed his lips to her brow fervently. "I've never been more proud or more terrified in my entire life."

Hal's face lifted, nuzzling against him. "I was so afraid for you."

"For me?" he asked as his fingers began to thread through her hair. "When you were the one facing a room filled with our enemies?"

"That was nothing," she whispered, her hands gripping at his coat, sliding towards his neck. "It was leaving without you that I couldn't bear. Not knowing…" She exhaled, the air dancing across his neck, sending shivers down his spine. "I'm never leaving without you again. I can't."

John groaned against her, the words echoing the sentiments that had haunted him all night. He tilted her face towards him, and his lips found hers almost at once. The contact stilled them both, heartbeats pounding between them, every sense attuning itself to that tenuous, powerful connection.

One of them sighed, possibly him, and then there was no hesitation, no pause. His lips molded to hers, blending with them in a heady fusion of familiarity and newness, dancing in a pattern that knew no tutor, needed no guidance. She arched into him, her hands pulling at his neck, fusing them together with an insistence that spurred him on. Yet her lips were tender and giving, generous in their attentions and gentle in their replies.

For it was a conversation between them, the revealing of every admiring look, every teasing smile, every moment of connection that had been steadily building. Words that could not be uttered were shared in each pass of lips, the stroke of each finger. This was no moment of sheer passion; it eclipsed anything that could be so easily written of, so lightly defined.

This was nothing like he had ever known, and nothing he would ever know again.

Slowly, gradually, and with grazing encores, the kisses began to fade, their hold on each other relaxing, their bodies softening against one another until they simply stood in the center of the room, holding each other without speaking.

There was something to be said for being held by the person one loved.

And even more for holding them yourself.

Hal sighed as she burrowed her face into his chest, her arms now loosely wrapped about his back. "How did you get out of there?"

John smiled, quite sure he would never be able to do anything else while holding her in his arms.

"Ruse," he murmured, his fingers running through her hair as his chin rested atop her head. "He knew the servants' corridors well and scuttled me out through them. Then we darted about the streets of Paris until we arrived home. I think there were some brutes sent after us, but I never saw for sure. You?"

"Skean." She leaned back just a little, smiling up at him. "The operative Ruse mentioned. It would seem he is quite familiar with my family and is rather an enigma. I liked him, once I decided to trust him. He bade me keep up my swooning spells, settled me into the parlor I was rumored to be in, and even convinced Jean that I was unwell. He posed as you for the Voclains' servants and brought me home in our coach. I hope you don't mind."

Chuckling, John kissed her softly. "Not at all, though I do hope he wasn't a better me than I am."

Hal lifted a brow and tightened her arms around him. "No one is a better you than you," she insisted, earning herself another kiss, this one lingering. "Mmm, I must say this is an improvement over our former state of marriage, Mr. Pratt."

"Happy to oblige, Mrs. Pratt." He touched his brow to hers, his delirium nearly overwhelming. "And I quite agree."

"Good." She rested against him for a moment, then nuzzled in and laid her head on his chest once more. "I am so tired, John. What a night!"

He rubbed his hands up and down her back in slow, soothing motions. "Go to bed, darling. Get some rest."

To his surprise, she shook her head. "No, I can't. Not yet." She sighed heavily but seemed to still against him. "I need to draw them."

"Now?" he asked in surprise.

He felt her nod. "Now. And we need to identify as many as we can as soon as possible. Can you write down all we heard while I begin?"

"Of course." He smiled as she yawned loudly. "And perhaps you need some coffee."

"Indeed," she quipped, though without her usual sprightliness. "And food, I think. We may be at this quite a while."

When Hal awoke, her head pounded miserably. Even through her still-closed eyes, she could feel every thump of her heartbeat, and it hurt.

Her mind slowly worked on the situation, blurred images from the night before coming into only slightly better focus. She'd been up for hours getting preliminary sketches done, she and John sitting quietly in their parlor, minds on their tasks. At some point, John had built up the fire and fetched them both some food from the kitchen, which she only recollected because he had brought a plate to her on the divan, then kissed the top of her head with tender affection.

She sighed now at the memory, stretching out in satisfaction on the bed. Who'd have thought that kissing her husband, and receiving his kisses, would have been so delightful? And who would ever have imagined that John Pratt would kiss so very well? They possessed the same single-minded intensity as every other task he took on, and there was such power in them, such heart…

It was enough to make one giddy.

And Hal was giddy.

And her head ached. Staying in bed longer than she already had would only leave her feeling more lethargic, which would not help matters. What ailed her was too much work into the wee hours of the morning and insufficient sleep to recover from it.

If the light streaming from beyond the curtains covering her windows was anything to go by, she had already slept far beyond her usual time. That was a clear indication of her fatigue if nothing else was.

Pulling herself out of bed, she dressed herself simply, though the gown she donned was still finer than anything she would have worn at home in London. Sprigged muslin had never been her choice over a comfortable calico, but there was an impression to maintain, and she would hate for word to somehow get back to Tilda that she had ignored her work. Besides, she felt slightly pretty in this particular shade of green, and it would be vastly entertaining to see if John thought so, too.

She loosely pinned her hair in the same haphazard style she usually did at home and ventured out of her bedchamber towards the main rooms of the house.

The growling of her stomach would have sent her directly for the breakfast room, though there might not have been anything of breakfast remaining for her, when she was distracted by the sounds of very young shrieks followed by a blend of adult and young laughter. Curious, and expecting her cousin to also have some unwritten rules about roughhousing with his children, Hal moved towards the noises that rendered the house so different from what its formal appearance would imply.

Nothing could have prepared her for the sight that met her eyes in the large drawing room where they had first met her cousins.

It was not, in fact, the Baron de Rouvroy who was playing with his rambunctious and jubilant children.

It was her husband.

John was on all fours, no jacket in sight, and he bore little Clara and Paul on his back while Sophie and Aimée darted around him, tiny little Marie struggling to keep up with her sisters. John chased after the girls, his steps exaggerated to the great delight of his riders. He suddenly lunged forward with a bark at Aimée's heels, making her yelp in surprise and sending Paul and Clara squealing as they clutched his shirt and waistcoat to maintain their position atop him.

Marie looked at John with some apprehension, her wide eyes turning almost luminous as she hid near the chair by which her sisters stood. She was a shy little one, and this stranger on all fours was clearly not putting her at ease in any way.

Sophie, the eldest of the young bunch, saw her sister's distress and crouched down beside her. "*Tout ma bien, ma chérie. Pourquoi tu ne caresses pas le chien?*"

Marie shook her head insistently.

Hal smiled at the ragtag group, hairbows askew, cheeks flushed, pinafores and shirts rumpled. All smiles but for Marie, and it warmed her heart to see John in the midst of them. Not just in the midst, but spurring them on and engaging with them. Where had her staid, proper, reserved husband gone and who was this lively, engaging, affable man in his place?

"*N'aie pas peur, Marie,*" Clara insisted, patting John on the head. "*Il est gentil!*"

Still, the little girl was not persuaded.

John eyed Marie for a moment, then imitated a convincing whimper and crept towards her. He lowered himself to the ground, the other children still on his back and giggling at the change in their incline. Then, of all things, he let his tongue loll out of his mouth and panted like a dog.

Hal covered her mouth to keep from laughing, and Marie's hesitant expression turned to one of curious delight. She took a few steps to close the distance between them, and, cautiously, batted his head twice.

Instantly, John keened a sound of encouragement, then slowly rolled to one side, effectively pinning Clara and Paul to the ground, which had them laughing uproariously as they attempted to free themselves. John nuzzled as close to Marie's legs as she would let him, and she cocked her head, now actually petting John and mussing his hair as she might a dog. Soon, John was on his back, arms and legs bent in the air, and all the children were scratching and petting the enormous dog they'd so recently been playing with.

Giggles erupted from all quarters, and Marie could even be heard to say, "*Bon chien.*"

"He will make a good father, *cousine.*"

Hal leaned against the wall just outside of the drawing room, smiling at her cousin, who had silently joined her. "Do you think so?"

Jean returned her smile and gestured to the room. "You don't?"

Hal looked back at John, her heart swelling at his antics, at his smile, at his willingness to let go of who he had been to spend this time with the children of his host. And to do it so well, despite all previous impressions and behaviors. There was so much more to this man she loved than she had ever suspected.

Her breath caught in her chest, her own thoughts repeating over and over again.

This man she loved.

Loved.

She loved John, and she loved him with a depth and breadth that startled her into silence. All she could do was stare at her husband and let herself feel just how much she loved him.

Her lips curved into a smile she couldn't resist. "I know," she murmured, the simple statement expressing far more than just the answer to her cousin's question.

Jean chuckled softly from his position. "It has been good for you both to be here, *ma chère*. I can see it in your eyes."

"Yes, it has." Hal nodded to herself, then glanced at her cousin with a sly smile. "And it was good for us to attend the opera alone. You were so good to let us use the box."

"Pah!" He waved off her gratitude dismissively. "Think nothing of it. As I said, I do not care for that opera anymore. Not everyone feels the same, but I cannot find enjoyment in it."

"Why not?" Hal asked, folding her arms gently into her wrap. "What changed?"

Jean offered her a rueful smile. "France."

"I don't understand," she responded, frowning.

"Yet it is simple enough." He shrugged one shoulder. "*Les Abencérages* was a favorite opera of Napoleon, you see. And his wife."

Hal stared at her cousin in shock, the significance of such a statement seeming to weigh down her very skirts. "Was it?"

Jean smiled, though it was flat and humorless. "It is said that his supporters flock to it regularly, though it cannot be used as a sign of support, obviously."

"Obviously." She blinked and wet her lips with hesitation. "Was that why you didn't attend with us?"

Her cousin nodded slowly. "I am not in a position to favor according to my opinions, unlike others in my country, Henrietta. I cannot risk my family. As such, despite no one in France being particularly pleased with a return to monarchy, many of us will support His Majesty. We will attend *Il viaggio a Reims* instead of *Les Abencérages*, not that we will be judged, but simply to remove any questions that may linger about us."

Hal shook her head slowly. "As particular as all that? Why accept royalty, then?"

"What choice did we have?" Jean asked, the sad excuse for a smile remaining. "We were a country exhausted, *ma chère*. Between *le Revolution* and Napoleon, almost no family was left untouched by death, loss, or war." He glanced up at the ceiling above them, the artistry a nostalgic memoir of the grandeur of France from long ago. "After the emperor was removed, and the Bourbons took over, French subjects were not treated well. It felt like being beat into submission, and those poor souls who had served in *la Grande Armée*…"

She should have left his trailing off where it was, but curiosity had never settled well with Hal, and so she ventured, "What happened?"

Jean brought his eyes back to her. "I think it was the late *Duc de Berry* who said, in your tongue, 'Let us go marshal hunting'. And Napoleon's marshals were indeed hunted. I do not know how successfully, but…" He only shrugged once more.

For all her devotion to England, Hal suddenly ached for her mother's country of France, and her family that still lived here.

And she wondered…

"It's a wonder you do not rise up again," she said before she could stop herself. "France, I mean."

Jean shook his head and straightened. "Someone likely will, should this manner continue. But I will not be among them. While His Majesty is not favored, his brother was fair enough. Monarchs come and monarchs go, *cousine*. You know this in England."

At this, Hal could only nod.

"And I," Jean went on with a sigh. "I do not possess the strength of character, or courage of conviction, to stray from the power most prevalent. I value my life, you see, and the lives of my family above *les parties intangibles de la vie*. For this, I am sometimes judged."

A furrow appeared between his thick brows, and Hal wondered just what sort of judgments he had faced in recent years, and from which quarters.

"But *mon Dieu connaîtra mon cœur*," he murmured almost to himself.

My God will know my heart.

It seemed to be a mantra as much as a prayer, a motto for his family, whatever tradition it had been. Surely, there could be no fault in such a statement. And surely, the Baron de Rouvroy was no traitor to his king or his country.

"And He shall be your judge," Hal replied, smiling gently.

Jean returned her smile and reached for her hand, kissing it softly. Then, the somber moment passed, and he laughed to himself. "So, I pray you will *pardonnes-moi, cousine,* if I cannot sing *Suspendez a ces murs* with you. Though I do not mind if you sing it, for the song is quite beautiful."

"Yes," Hal agreed with a laugh and a nod. "Yes, it was quite stirring."

Something in her mind clicked and spun, playing the song in question at twice the speed, the lyrics echoing with a startling clarity.

That song. Those words.

Vous ne me verrez pas mourir…

That was it.

"Holy blessed heavens…" Hal breathed, reaching for the wall beside her with one hand. She swallowed hard, feeling the color draining from her cheeks and did not need her cousin's concerned expression to tell her so.

"Henrietta?" he asked, immediately looking her over. "You look ill again. I had hoped your rest would have cured you." He turned to the drawing room. "Pratt, I fear Henrietta is unwell once more."

John was to her in an instant, the groans of the children audible.

"*Ange*?" he murmured, taking her arms and giving her a thorough look. "What is it?"

Hal stared at him in horror and awe, her thoughts not quite concise enough to express, and certainly not before such company. "I think… I think I need to place a candle in our window."

Chapter Thirteen

"Tell me what you're thinking."

"I think you might be the most brilliant mind in England *and* France."

"Hardly. I'm married to you."

John turned in his seat to give his wife an amused look. "Meaning what, exactly?"

Hal's eyes widened, and she tossed her head back on a laugh, one of her naturally curled tendrils tumbling from the hold she'd placed them in earlier. "I didn't mean that!"

"I'd be most interested to hear what you *did* mean, then," John pressed, grinning in the face of her delighted laughter.

There would never be a more beautiful sight to him than that. Never.

"I meant that I could never be brilliant when compared to *you*, John." She shook her head, her expression now turning exasperated. "I do not doubt that if you had heard Jean, you'd have leapt to the exact same conclusions as I did, and you undoubtedly would already know how to apply them."

"I still believe you are the more brilliant one." He shrugged and leaned his arm on the back of the chair, lacing his fingers together. "I have no complaints about it, my pride is not in the least offended."

Hal snorted softly. "Well, that is a relief. I was so concerned about your pride. Besides," she paused, situating herself on the divan in their parlor with a sigh, rolling herself to one side to face him more fully, "I couldn't be the most brilliant mind in France. They are the ones who devised this system, whatever it is."

John exhaled a heavy sigh of disappointment, still smiling. "Always determined to minimize your brilliance, *Ange*."

"Have you met me, John? I never minimize anything I do." She flashed an impish grin that made him positively mad to kiss her senseless.

"No," he murmured slowly, pushing out of his chair and moving towards her, "nor should you, by heaven. All should be in awe of you, as I am."

Her eyes darkened, her smile deepening. "Are you, indeed? Well, well, Mr. Pratt, what do you intend to do in the face of your awestruck state?"

One of his brows quirked at her blatant teasing, and he leaned close to her. "I've an idea or two…"

A knock at their parlor door had them both groaning.

"Infernal interruptions," Hal grumbled, her expression souring. "What could not wait but five minutes more?"

John chuckled. "It'll keep, *Ange*." He closed the gap between them and kissed her quickly, pulling away when she arched in for more. "Now, now," he scolded with a warning look, though his legs were presently on fire for her.

Hal scowled further and moved herself to a more proper position on the divan. "We need to have a serious discussion about your priorities, Mr. Pratt."

"I welcome the discussion the moment it is appropriate, Mrs. Pratt." He opened the parlor door, politely smiling at the footman there. "Yes?"

"A parcel has arrived for you, monsieur," the heavily accented voice intoned, extending a gold tray out to him with the wrapped package atop.

John nodded and removed the parcel, his pulse lurching with sudden anticipation. "*Merci*."

"And *le baron* wishes to know if Madame Pratt is feeling improved?"

A wry smile crossed John's lips. "She is resting at the present, but I daresay she will be well enough to join us for supper this evening. Please thank the baron for his concern."

The footman bowed in acceptance, snapping his heels together, then moved back down the corridor to deliver his message.

"Next time, inquire as to the menu for supper before promising that I shall attend," Hal suggested as he closed the door. "My wellness may depend on it."

John gave her a look as he moved back to the table, tearing the paper off the parcel. He replied with a noncommittal humph.

She swung her legs down from the divan and pushed up to join him. "Did he get it?"

There was no need to respond, as she could see for herself.

The music to *Suspendez a ces murs* was in hand, and now the true test could begin.

"Remind me to ask the Shopkeepers to increase whatever they are paying Ruse," John murmured as his eyes darted from note to note and word to word on the page. "Perhaps even double it."

Hal wrapped her arm around his and leaned her head on his shoulder. "Let's see if this works first. Where will you begin?"

John's mouth curved on one side. "I have already begun. The moment we returned here, and you placed the candle in the window, I tried the letters using that phrase uttered at the meeting. *Vous ne me verrez pas mourir.*"

"And?"

"And the difficulty with deciphering is that one cannot know one's success until the whole puzzle reveals itself." He turned his face and kissed the top of her head. "But I think the music might be the key."

Hal stroked his arm gently in response. "Why is that?"

"Hard to say." He eyed the music again, nodding to himself. "This feels right. I cannot explain any further than that, I'm afraid."

"I don't need further than that. Let's go to work."

John glanced at her as she left his side and pulled out another chair from the table. "You're going to help?"

Hal gave him a quizzical look. "Yes… You have quite a number of letters there, and we will be trying a number of solutions to get that damned code to reveal itself. I can follow instructions well, so tell me what to do." To emphasize the point, she sat and placed her hands in her lap, waiting for him to follow.

He'd had help before, this was no novelty, but more often than not, he preferred working in solitude, thought more clearly without assistance or spectators.

This, however, he felt he could do with ease.

"Very well, *Ange*," he murmured taking his seat once more. "First, let's look at the song."

Hal nodded once. "Why?"

John laid the music down and smiled in near exasperation. "Why? Are you going to question the entire process?"

"Not questioning," she replied without a hint of amusement or ruffling. "Inquiring. Why do you want to look at the song?"

Her curious mind was really something of a wonder, and he had no qualms about satiating it however he could.

"Because," he explained, pulling a letter and one of his discarded attempts at deciphering it over, "it is clear to me, from the errors so far, that there is a layered aspect to their code. You were clever enough to see significance in the opera Napoleon loved and that our Faction friends quoted. It seems to me that there is something about this song that resonates with them, and if it were only a matter of words, I should have seen some pattern already."

A puckered furrow appeared between her brows as she craned her neck to look at the letter again. "But there are any number of phrases from the song that could have been used. How do you know?"

John reached for the music again and searched for the phrase he needed before pointing at it. "Because everything has meaning to the Faction. Why else would they have chosen that exact phrase to recite in response to the usual Sieyès quote? People love hidden meanings, *Ange*, and we are dealing with a group of quite dedicated idealists."

Hal nodded repeatedly, now looking at the music with him. "So, what would we use in this song, if we were them?"

"Well," he said on an exhale, letting his eyes rove the page at will, "I've seen music used before, mostly taking familiar tunes and changing them somehow to suit the needs of a code. This, however, strikes me as something rather pure to our friends, so I cannot believe they would alter it…"

His words trailed off as he began laying out the pages of the song, tracking here and there for ideas and options, the melody floating in and out of memory out of sheer habit. But there had to be something obvious, else new additions to the Faction's circle would struggle immensely with communication.

Unless all communication was only exchanged between important members.

Not that such a level of significance had much relevance here. Any of the members could have copies of the music at their residences, much as they did here, and simply followed the pattern for deciphering as laid out.

But what *was* the pattern, and how could he find it?

"Do you read music, John?" Hal asked after a moment, her voice somehow seeming far away.

He nodded absently. "Rather well, as it happens. Jeremy took more pains to dance to music, while I was far more interested in playing it. Mother wanted us both tutored in music, but Jeremy would have none of it."

"Do you sing?"

"Not at all." He smiled but kept his eyes on the music. "I hope that doesn't disappoint you."

Hal laughed and took a letter from the stack to review. "I believe I will recover."

John went back to the first page and looked at every mark thereon. The description of emotion of a part, the notations on volume, each phrase that repeated itself in lyrics. Still, none of that answered his questions.

What was he looking for? What could they…?

"Could they?" he murmured to himself, returning to the beginning of the song as an idea struck him. "Why not? Simple, yet effective, and not plain to the naked eye…" He found himself nodding as he studied each note in turn, almost as though he intended to memorize the melody for his own enjoyment. "And does it change…?" He plucked the other sheets up and ran his eyes over them.

Hal sat silently beside him, but he could feel her attention on him, could almost feel the same excitement he felt rising in her.

"Yes," he whispered, circling his find with a finger. "Brilliant. Right before the eyes, in plain sight, and yet so easily missed…"

A fresh sheet of paper was slid under his left hand, and he glanced at the disruption before looking up at his wife, whose smile brought on one of his own.

She tilted her head to the page. "It seems you've got it. Go to it."

He could have kissed her but settled for taking the paper and pen and jotting down his discovery.

"It's the music," he said aloud as he wrote, looking between the notes and his page as he copied everything down. "The actual music itself. The time signature is the letter number, in this case, every fourth. The key signature is the key letter, so as we start, this is D."

"But it changes so quickly," Hal pointed out, tapping the page where the key signature changes. "So, the key letter would change as well?"

John nodded, now scribbling away. "Yes. C, in that instance. Now, the distance each note is from the major key letter is the number of letters away from whatever letter is written. Here. The key note is C, and this note is D, which places the corresponding letter of the code as one letter advanced of what we see." He frowned to himself, tilting his head at the music. "Sharps… flats… Likely as obvious as the rest, so a sharp added to a note would be an additional one ahead, and a flat would be one behind. That would mean a natural sign would correspond with whatever it does to the note in that key signature. If the note is sharped in the key signature, it would be one ahead, if it's flatted, it would be one behind. Does that make sense?"

He laughed softly to himself, shaking his head. "Marvelous coding. Genius, really. Change in key signature changes the key letter value, but the principle is the same. And here," he paused to tap the initial find that had settled him on this code as the right one. "A time signature change would indicate a change of which letter we must identify; here, it means we go to every third letter."

For a long moment, the only sound was that of the nib of his pen scratching away at the page before him, and then he paused again, his mind spinning.

"What?" Hal's question was faint but insistent.

Poor lamb, she likely had no idea what he was talking about as yet; he was barely making sense to himself. But this was his process, and though he spoke his findings aloud, his explanation wasn't exactly thorough.

"But what about the value of each note?" he murmured, staring blankly at the music again. "In each measure, the note itself… That could add a new dimension…"

Hal's hand suddenly covered the music. "John," she said sternly, taking his chin in hand and forcing him to look at her. "Anyone would already have to spend hours in an attempt to code this. We cannot assume that everyone in the Faction has a brilliant mind like yours. Kindly don't give them more credit than they deserve, and just see if this works."

John searched her eyes, the tension of frustrated efforts coiling in his chest. Then, to his surprise, it relaxed and enabled him to breathe as well as smile. "You're right."

"I know," she quipped, patting his cheek, "but it is good practice for you to say so."

He chuckled and leaned in to give her a quick kiss. "Impudent."

"Always."

He winked and returned his focus to the mountain of work they now had before them. "Right. Time to go code hunting."

Hours later, including a reprieve for supper with the de Rouvroys, John continued staring at the pages before him, the jumble of letters still not offering clues as to the next layer of code.

They'd deciphered every letter Hal had copied from Leclerc's pocket using the music, and yet, they were somehow far from answers. Closer than they had been before, it was true, but now he was back at the beginning of the process once more.

And his mind was tired.

It wasn't often he could claim that, as he had worked on a number of cases and ciphers in his career with the Home and Foreign Offices, the War Office, and the individual groups such as the Garden, the London League, and special missions from the Convent.

This was his forte, his strength, his gift, and his calling. This was what he offered to the Crown as a show of his loyalty and fidelity.

And he was tired.

He sat back in his chair roughly, shaking his head at himself. There was very little more he could do without the cipher for this next layer, and until he had some proper rest, he would not find the strength or capacity to discover it. There was nothing to indicate that any of these messages were time-sensitive or crucial to England or her interests, so he could only hope and pray that nothing would be risked by his pausing the process.

Surely, there was room for him to be human.

John blinked and looked across the room where Hal dozed on the divan, her head tucked down as it laid against the armrest, her body curved into itself. She'd changed out of her supper finery some time ago, though he was still dressed in his. His cravat was long gone, and the buttons at his throat were undone, his jacket slung over the chair, but in all other respects, he was dressed the same.

Somehow, John hadn't been much aware of Hal's change in attire, so focused was he on his work. She'd donned her nightgown and worn a dressing gown over it, cinched at the waist and entirely modest. Still, there was something stirring about the woman he loved in her nightgown, hair completely loosed and magnificent about her shoulders, remaining out in this parlor with him while he worked rather than seeking the comfort of her bed.

She'd done what she could to help him with the decryption, proving herself quite useful in the more menial and time-consuming task of applying the code to each letter. Then, when that had all been done, she had encouraged his thinking aloud at what the next layer could be, challenged him to think deeper, reach further, and expand his possibilities wider than he possibly had ever done before.

She was a magnificent wonder, his wife, and he had no understanding of how he might deserve her.

Sighing with exhaustion, John rose from his chair, stretching out his back and groaning at the pain there, then shaking out each leg as it cramped, protesting his rising. He yawned and paced about the room for a moment, stopping at Hal's sketches, all laid out on the floor.

She must have pulled them out at some point while he was whittling away at the words of each letter. The likenesses of each were startling, and, but for two or three, John could identify each one. Some slight color had been added to each, if for no other reason than to indicate the coloring of each man, but the features were unmistakable.

They had names and faces, and hopefully soon, they would have words as well. But what did they want? What were their aims?

And why did those aims include England?

Oh, he had no doubt that there would have been operatives in France had the interests only extended there, purely to keep an eye on things and keep significant parties informed. They'd done so during the Revolution, in fact, which had been of real value to England herself. Eagle had been one of the chief operatives there, and Weaver, too, though he had been coded Fox at the time.

Weaver would have been in the very earliest days of his operative career. What an assignment to be given so young!

Had that been why he had sent Hal to France now? The face of France had changed greatly since then, but there were likely some things that remained the same. Weaver could not function as an operative himself now, not being so public a dignitary and almost-ambassador to all of Europe, but he could very likely still have interest in certain members of France. Had he wanted to see faces he might know from missions long ago?

It wouldn't make much difference, John supposed as he stepped back to look at the sketches on the whole. Weaver had long proven his selflessness when it came to England, and if he had suspicions that had been founded from previous missions, they would be well-founded now.

A soft sound from behind him brought John around, and he smiled as Hal shifted sleepily on the divan.

He moved there and gently scooped her up into his arms, pressing his lips gently to her brow as she nuzzled into him. "Come on, *Ange*," he murmured. "Time for bed."

"Come with me," she mumbled as she nestled more comfortably into his chest. "Sleep, too."

He chuckled and carried her towards her bedchamber. "I will, love. In a bit."

"Now," she insisted, though there was no force to her words.

"I will, but in my bed tonight. We both need sleep." He entered her darkened room and paused, letting his eyes adjust.

Hal harrumphed and adjusted her head on his shoulder. "I *will* sleep. I don't know what you were thinking."

"Of course," he chuckled, kissing her brow once more. "Neither do I."

His wife hummed almost dreamily in his arms. "I didn't think you were strong enough to carry me anywhere. No offense intended."

Now John hefted her more securely in his arms, just to prove his strength. "Well, remember what Ruse said? Nothing in Paris is as it appears…" He trailed off, stiffening, lost in thought.

Nothing was as it appeared… An opera favored by Napoleon. Many members in attendance, not for enjoyment but for solidarity. Reminders. Rejuvenation. To hear the words they so valued.

The song had the key to unlock the code. The words hadn't been, but the song.

Which left words.

Words…

Faction words.

Words.

J'ai vécu.

John blinked at the realization, his breath vanishing from his lungs. That was it.

That was *it.*

Hal shifted, looking up at him. He looked back at her, beyond speaking at this moment, the significance too great. He saw understanding reflected in her eyes, though she wouldn't have known the reason.

She glanced down at the proximity between their position and the bed, pursing her lips. It was right there, just a half step away.

Slowly, she looked back up at him, expression wary. "You wouldn't dare…"

John grinned a rather wolfish grin at his wife. "Oh no?"

"John…"

Without a second thought, John tossed her onto the bed, the downy depths nearly swallowing her whole, and he dashed back out of the room into the parlor, his epiphany all-consuming.

Hal's near-hysterical laughter echoed behind him, filling his ears with the joyous sound.

He nearly joined in the laughter, though his would have been from sheer exhilaration.

J'ai vécu.

The statement of allegiance, loyalty, or sympathies used by the Faction for the past couple of years should have been the obvious choice for a cipher. Should have occurred to him long ago. He'd even tried that as a key when he'd first worked the letters, though the first layer hadn't allowed him any revelations from it.

It would seem that the members of the Faction were sentimental as well as idealists. Nothing was as it appeared, but everything was significant.

He yanked all the letters to him, eyes darting over each page and every letter. It could work. It *had* to work.

"Paper, paper, paper…" he muttered, tossing aside the music and pages of random scratches he had made trying to decipher things earlier.

"Here, love." Hal brought a stack of pages from her belongings and set them before him. She wrapped her arms about his neck and leaned in, kissing his cheek. "You're the most brilliant mind in England and France," she whispered against his skin, "and bloody likely everywhere else, too."

Heat burst into showers of sparks in his stomach, the combination of her endearment, her lips, and her claim rendering him speechless. He turned his head and kissed her hard, one of his hands reaching for the back of her head.

It was a kiss for the ages, for centuries to come, for eons of breathless moments between them. He poured everything of himself into it, exhilaration, energy, excitement, and hope, until he was vulnerable and raw in her arms, nothing hidden from the goddess who held his heart. And she gave him everything and more, sighing into his mouth, her lips molding with his, her fingers toying with his hair.

Was there anything God had ever made that was more perfect than this?

Hal broke off, humming and breathless, cupping his cheek with one hand while the other stayed playfully in his hair. She smiled, keeping her brow and nose against his. "A marked improvement in those priorities of yours, Mr. Pratt." She sighed unsteadily, which nearly undid him. "I do believe, however, there is something quite pressing to attend to." She tilted her head playfully. "Other than your wife, I mean."

"More's the pity," he whispered, brushing his lips against hers in the barest hint of a graze that sent them both shivering. "Care to be my assistant?"

That earned him a quick, but firm kiss. "Love to. But first, coffee." She quirked her brows and slid her arms from him, heading for the door.

"Make it drinking chocolate," he called after her with a smile. "It is Paris, after all."

Hal gave him a jaunty salute and a wink, then wrenched open the door and hurried out.

John shook his head, then returned his attention to the papers before him, fatigue gone and only anticipation remaining. "All right, then," he said to the collection. "Now, let's see what secrets you contain…"

Chapter Fourteen

"This is… I don't even… Erm…"

Hal grinned and looked up at her husband. "If I ever doubted his nationality, that alone would do it. I vow, the most British utterance known to man is 'erm'. There is nothing like it."

John only chuckled, nodding as he leaned against the tree by which they stood.

Ruse didn't seem to hear her or note John's reaction. He simply stared, his eyes on nothing, looking as blank as the character he was portraying. "Damn…"

"And that would be the second most British utterance." Hal clapped her hands in delight and returned her attention to the book she was supposed to be reading in this interview. "Marvelous, Ruse. I feel quite at home."

"Glad to oblige." He looked between the two of them, eyes round. "So, it's only the three you mentioned that you can't name?"

"I can't see that we ever were introduced," John answered with a slight tsk. "*Ange*?"

The name instantly curved her lips into a smile, such sweetness being ascribed to it now. "No," she agreed, keeping her tone mild. "No, I've never seen them. I've provided copies for you in that basket. Perhaps you can make quick work of it, I couldn't think of a feasible way to bring them to my cousin for his help."

"No, no, I concur." Ruse took a bite of the apple he'd taken from the basket, bowing himself before them in a show of gratitude, though he was already sitting on the ground near Hal. "Do you realize what this means? Any correspondence we get our hands on we can now interpret. This puts us at a great advantage compared to where we have been."

"That was the idea of sending us here, was it not?" Hal glanced over at their companion, unable to keep the satisfied smile from her face. "The transcript of the meeting is also there. We've given you a copy as well as the packet to get back to England."

Ruse nodded, though he didn't seem quite as relaxed about the thing as John or Hal did. "*Merci beaucoup.*"

Hal frowned at the thanks, given the flatness of the tone. She looked up at John, who was also frowning.

"What is it?" John asked in a low tone, almost threatening in his manner.

"Operatives," Ruse replied at once. He shook his head slowly. "That was the word, yes?"

John looked down at the ground, no doubt thinking back. "*Agents*," he recited. "Nothing specific about them, but they were mentioned."

"Not *espions*?" Ruse prodded.

"No," Hal confirmed, laying down her book once more. "Why? Is there a significance between an operative, agent, and a spy?"

Ruse met her eyes, the most serious he had ever been in her presence. "Possibly not. That's the problem. You both were operatives before you received this assignment, in a way. We might say asset, but an operative all the same."

Hal nodded, seeing the logic in that, and thinking she could see where his thoughts were taking him. "Agreed."

"But a spy," he went on, "would be someone more like Trace or Trick. Actively in the face of danger, transplanted from their usual life and surroundings." He offered a humorless smile. "Rather like the two of you now, I suppose."

"And you," John pointed out.

Ruse shrugged. "I didn't have much of a life in England as it was. It is all relative, in my case. Home is England, but more than that, I have no ties. Which is likely why I've been here as long as I have."

"How long is that?" Hal found herself asking. "If you don't

mind."

"Five years." His smile turned a little whimsical, his eyes lowering. "I did have a cousin, though. I do have one, I suppose. She must think I abandoned her like everyone else in her life. I am sorry for that, but Weaver assures me Clara is safe."

Hal cocked her head, looking over Ruse's features and calling upon a memory she'd long since tucked away. "Clara Harlow?"

Ruse's eyes widened, and he reared back. "How the devil…"

"Steady," John hissed as he shifted towards them, somehow still keeping his casual pose. "Her memory, remember?"

"Right." Ruse swallowed, clearly unnerved. "Sorry. But how?"

Hal smiled with as much gentleness as she could find within her. "I can see the similarity in features. On my last visit to the Convent, I met her. She doesn't know what it is, of course, but she is well liked by the girls. Teaches French, I believe, and perhaps dance?"

"She would." A quick, but genuine smile flashed across his face, making him seem years younger. "If I were to give you a note for her, would you see it reaches her when you return to England? I'd rather not use our channels for personal means."

"I'd be delighted." Hal smiled in return, finding a lump in her throat difficult to remove.

What if her brother had been sent out of England for an assignment? He would likely not be able to communicate with her as readily as he did now, and Hal would feel abandoned as well, though she had never been particularly cast out by Society. What did Miss Harlow endure in her heart if her closest relation did not maintain the connection between them, especially when she did not know the reason why?

It was painful even to imagine.

"Incoming," John murmured into the silence that had stretched, his eyes on figures in the distance.

Hal looked, nodding as she resumed reading her book once more. "So, when do you anticipate a response, Ruse?"

"Quickly, I'd think." He made a show of taking things from the basket and putting them in his pockets. "I can have this to Calais tonight, across the Channel and into necessary hands by luncheon tomorrow. I'd say a response should be due to you in three days, perhaps four." He shrugged as the packet slipped into a pouch behind his back, hiding beneath the filthy tunic he wore over equally tattered additional layers. "A week at most, if they need to think on it."

John grunted once. "A week in Paris."

Something in his voice drew Hal's attention and she looked up at him, heart skipping.

His eyes were on her, heat and adoration and promise swirling in them, the curve of his smile practically hypnotic. "Whatever shall we do?"

Heavens…

Hal managed a smile in return, her stomach clenching. "I'm sure we'll think of something."

"Right," Ruse said slowly, looking between the two. "I'll leave you to whatever unspoken message is taking place there and thank you both profusely for what you've done."

John broke their heated gaze first, smiling with genuine cordiality at their contact, and in many ways, protector. "Our pleasure. Truly. And if we find any ways to help while we await further instructions, we will do so."

"Might I suggest you and your companions practice playing faro?" Hal offered. "There was an actual card game taking place during the meeting, so it could prove useful."

Ruse suddenly looked intrigued. "How did you know it was faro? By your own account, you were only in the room a minute or two."

Hal gave him a sardonic look. "I do know the difference between faro, commerce, and *vingt-et-un*, thank you, and I cheat successfully in all three."

Both John and Ruse chuckled at that.

"I have no doubt, Sketch." Ruse tapped his cap with a finger and nodded at them both. "I'll send word when I have it." He turned and tottered away, his shuffling gait negating anything youthful one might have seen in his face.

Hal shook her head as she watched him go. "What a bewildering person."

"I do believe you've just described every operative known to man," John told her, coming to her side and offering a hand. "If you've had enough of reading in the sun, my dear, perhaps we might stroll homeward?"

"Oh, why not?" Hal snapped her book shut and slid it into the basket they'd brought as a show for Ruse, then placed her hand in John's, letting him pull her up.

John smiled at her, rubbing his hands along her arms. "Well, we've just handed over the culmination of several weeks' work to be delivered to our superiors. How do you feel?"

Hal exhaled slowly, letting the feelings of this entire venture wash over her. "Relieved. Tired. Worried."

"Worried?" he repeated. "About what?"

"Nothing so serious," she assured him, looping her hand through his arm and letting him walk them out of the park. "Little things. What if they already know of the men we identified? What if my drawings aren't accurate enough?"

"*Ange*, really…" John scoffed. "They could have stood for those portraits for hours and no one would know the difference."

Hal inclined her head, accepting the compliment without actually acknowledging it. "Even so, there is a chance." She made a face, her fingers absently rubbing against his arm. "What if what we sent wasn't enough? What if we've missed something? What if…?"

"What if we've just delivered exactly what they were looking for?" he overrode with his unwavering calmness. "What if we've exceeded expectations? What if we become the new partnership to beat in the covert world?"

A startled laugh burst from Hal's lips, and she covered her eyes to hide her mirth. "Oh, please…"

"I don't see why it's so far-fetched." John covered her hand with his as they turned the corner. "There are a million things that could be decided now, and there is no point in overthinking it. I meant what I said back there to Ruse. We will continue to do what we can. For all we know, we could be here another four months working on the same thing, digging deeper and finding more to aid the rest."

That was a sobering thought. Not a dismal one, by any stretch, but sobering all the same. She'd always thought this would be a short-term assignment, but if they proved especially useful, why wouldn't they be retained?

"We'd have to take a house, if that was the case," she murmured, smiling to herself. "I adore my relations, but one does wish for privacy."

"Hell yes," John grunted with a squeeze of her hand that made her giggle. Then he turned serious once more. "Or they could send us back to England tomorrow. We just don't know, and I don't think it serves either of us to worry about that."

Hal made a noncommittal sound of consideration. "I suppose not."

Back to England.

There wasn't quite the same sense of relief and warmth in that statement as there might have been at the beginning of all this. Oh, she would love to return to a quieter life, to be sure, but returning meant a return to the way things had been. She and John need not be married. Would no longer be partners. Would have no reason to be.

The plan for the annulment could commence.

Perhaps it wouldn't work, as had been suggested was possible. Perhaps it would not be as simple a matter as Tailor and Weaver had described. Perhaps something could go horribly wrong and the marriage license Priest had secured disappeared, thus preventing its destruction.

Once they returned to England, it was entirely possible she would no longer be Mrs. Pratt.

Suddenly, the mission and its fallout were not her most pressing concerns at all, had no place in her Hall of Worries, did not matter so much as a jot.

Her marriage to John and its longevity were now her most imperative concerns.

But what did he want? What could he be thinking there? Did he love her with the same fervor which she did him? If his kisses were anything to go by, he was not displeased with her. If the change in his manner towards her, the sweetness of his expression, the tenderness in his touch conveyed anything of what lay beneath the surface, she might have reason to hope.

Hope.

Such a thing had never really been part of her nature or her life, but suddenly hope was all she knew.

All she had.

And hope lived in every finger that clung to John's arm as they walked slowly home.

Had the meeting with Ruse gone on any longer, John might have gone completely mad. There was too much at stake for him to have any interest in hypothesizing the plans of the Shopkeepers or the intentions of the Faction in their letters. All those details could be left to those who would have the authority and interest to act upon them, not to those individuals designated to bring the information to light.

All he wanted was to return home, return to their parlor, and wait for his curious wife to stumble upon the one thing that had occupied his mind from the moment he'd finished decrypting the letters. The moment he'd realized what his success, and hers, would mean.

The end of their mission could be at hand, and while he wouldn't mind leaving the danger behind, there was one thing that he would absolutely refuse to abandon.

His wife.

His *Ange*.

His chest had been seized with an almost panic when it had occurred to him that this all could come to an end rather quickly. Neither of them had wanted this marriage on the onset, only entered into it out of necessity for the mission and at the behest of their leaders.

It was so much more than that now. So much had changed, and the idea that it could all go back to the way it was did not sit well with him. Was unimaginable.

Was unacceptable.

Could not be.

Would not, if he had anything to say about it.

So, in the morning hours, before his wife had woken from the limited sleep they would both receive after yet another late night of work, he'd set about on a completely separate project. One that now awaited them and could dictate the whole course of his future.

Clearly, nothing to be concerned about.

She had to love him; she *had* to. She could not have gone from nearly despising him to kissing him with such ardor and not have it be love. No one was so convincing an actress, especially not Henrietta Mortimer.

Pratt, he reminded himself, a wave of panic hitting him. She was Henrietta Pratt, and he prayed she always would be.

Oh, heavens, what if she didn't want to be?

He swallowed with some difficulty as they reentered the de Rouvroy home and found the place completely silent.

Odd.

"Ze family 'ave all gone to Madame Moreau," the butler explained as he approached, seeing their confused expressions. "All but Monsieur René, who 'as gone to ze club with his friends."

"*Merci*," Hal murmured, stripping off her gloves and handing them over with a smile.

John said nothing and simply let the man take his hat.

"A quiet house," Hal mused when they were alone again, smiling in that impish way he loved so well. "Shall we sneak about the house and find all of the places we have yet to see? Perhaps unearth a secret inheritance I have been owed. You could actually receive something of a dowry for marrying me!" She laughed and nearly skipped down the corridor as though she were going to do just that.

He'd die where he stood if he had to endure aimless wandering about the house just to pass the time.

"No," he said brusquely, wincing in his mind at the tone the simple word adopted.

Hal turned and gave him a surprised look. "I was only teasing."

"I know." He tried for a smile but failed miserably. "Forgive me, I am tired, and the rest I received did not make up for the night I passed."

She smiled with some sympathy and came back to him. "I can understand that. Why not go upstairs and rest? At least get rid of this." She flicked the ends of his cravat out from his waistcoat, quirking a brow. "I like you better without it anyway."

John almost groaned and took her waist in hand. "Come with me? You must be fatigued, too."

"Oh, I am." On cue, she yawned, covering her mouth with the back of her hand. "Pardon me. I am, to be sure. But I am also famished. So, you go on up, and I'll fetch us a tray of something, then follow presently."

Heaven and angels, this was surely some test of his will and patience.

But he smiled, nodded, and moved for the stairs to do just that, remembering belatedly that he hadn't kissed her then.

Damnation, she might read something into that.

There was nothing to do but continue up to their rooms, remove his cravat, and lay on his bed and wait.

Once there, and all that accomplished, he settled in to wait, though rest was far from his mind. His heart pounded with the fury of a thousand thunderstorms, and every sense was attuned to the door of the parlor. Conveniently, that door happened to be in view from his present position, if he kept his adjoining door open wide.

Which it presently was.

At long last, the parlor door opened, and Hal entered, kicking the door shut behind her.

He'd have laughed at such antics if he didn't feel so frantic at the moment.

"I find the kitchen staff most accommodating," Hal called as she set the tray down on the table. "I daresay if I asked for a three-tiered cake, one would be produced from a storeroom somewhere. You would not believe what I have… What's this?"

The rustle of paper on the table sent a sharp pang of anticipation to John's heart, and strangely jolting something into the sole of his left foot.

"John, what is this?" she asked, her steps coming closer.

He pried open one eye, though in truth they had not been fully closed at any point. "That? Oh, I thought you might wish for more practice with your deciphering skills. Given all the experience you now have, it seemed prudent to at least continue to see you trained. I worked that up for you while you slept."

"Did you?" she mused, smiling at the note, then up at him, her fair eyes dancing. "It's complete gibberish."

"It is not," he insisted with a smile of his own. "It is coded. Very much not gibberish, if you will work it out."

Hal rocked from her toes to her heels and back again, a child-like enthusiasm emanating from her. "All right, I will. And we shall see how brilliant your wife is, Mr. Sphinx." She turned on her heel and scampered to the table, pulling out one of the blank sheets nearby and setting to work.

"Right," he heard her say, both eyes fully open now as he watched her hunch over her work. "What have we here?"

He fought a smile, wishing he could see her face better, but content enough if she would keep speaking her thoughts aloud.

"A replacement cipher?" she mused to no one in particular. "Or whatever one calls it. That seems most logical… Which means… Hmm…"

John quietly sat up, watching her with interest, unable to keep from smiling.

"No…" Hal suddenly shook her head and crossed something out. "Not simple replacement. Close, though. I need a word, and then it should be clear…"

There she was, and he was proud to see her process working through it.

He foresaw a great deal of amusement in various puzzles in their future if all went well.

"Oh," he heard her half-gasp. "Oh, that's… Yes, that's…"

His heart stopped for a beat. *The key.*

He'd hoped she'd have got that first rather than guess a word in the body of the note itself. The key would unlock everything, after all.

Ange.

There was nothing else it could have been.

Nothing else *she* could have been.

Slowly, silently, he swung his legs from the bed and pushed up, rising and walking very carefully to the doorway, leaning against it while she worked.

"*Ange*," she recited, her pen scratching out the letters. "I…" Her lips moved, but no sound came from them.

John held his breath, watching, waiting…

Hal blinked, the pen clattering from her fingers onto the table, then looked up at him, her lips parted.

He managed a small smile but said nothing.

She blinked again, then shoved her chair back and bolted to him in a matter of three strides, her hands flying to his face. She kissed him hard, deeply and emphatically, and it was all he could do to fix his arms around her to keep them both upright and steady.

"I love you, too," she whispered when she took a breath, tears tracing down her cheeks to her lips. "Oh, I love you."

John kissed her again, more tenderly but no less thoroughly, holding her close. "*Ange*, I love you, I adore you, I need you…" He shook his head, kissing her once more.

Hal whimpered against his mouth, pressing herself closer to him. "I wanted this. I wanted *you.* John…" She exhaled and dropped her head, resting it against his chin. "I love you."

Chuckling with relief, John tilted his face to kiss her brow. "And the rest?"

"The rest?" she repeated, pulling back to look at him in confusion.

"Did you leave the message incomplete?" He laughed again, this time in disbelief. "*Ange*!"

"I thought I'd gotten far enough," she protested as she looped her arms about his neck.

He raised a brow at that. "What if I followed that with the word but?"

Hal was completely nonplussed by the threat. "Did you?"

"No."

She shrugged. "Then I don't see a problem."

Blast, but he loved this woman, and there was no doubt she would test him for the rest of their days.

"There was more," he told her, dipping his voice low, leaning close.

Hal arched up and pressed her brow to his, stroking the nape of his neck with one hand. "Tell me what it says."

John hesitated, not out of apprehension, but out of painful hope. He closed his eyes, his hold on her tightening.

"Stay my wife?"

He heard her rough exhale, could feel the breath of it against his lips. Then, she tilted her face and brought her lips to his in the softest, most breathless caress he could have imagined, robbing him of strength, sense, and stamina.

"Yes," she breathed, nuzzling her lips against his. "Yes."

He took her lips more firmly, more securely, sealing their promise as though this day, this moment, were their wedding, not the formality of weeks before.

This was their birth and beginning.

Here and now, choosing one another.

Loving one another.

"Thank you," he managed when they parted, grazing his lips along her cheek in absent adoration.

Hal laughed softly, the sound almost dreamy. "You're quite welcome. After all, a lifetime with you is a right sight better than the chance of damnation."

John paused in his shower of kisses and dropped his face to her shoulder as he snorted a laugh. "Well," he told her as he straightened, cupping her cheek, "at least I know that about myself. Better than damnation. I've always wanted to be described as such."

His brilliant, beautiful wife beamed up at him. "I've already given you several compliments of late, Mr. Pratt. One would like to keep one's husband from growing too proud or too arrogant."

"Keep me however you like, Mrs. Pratt," he said with a smile in return, "so long as I stay in your keeping."

"You will. I'm quite a possessive woman."

"Poor me."

"Indeed, yes. Poor you."

And then he kissed her again, and for quite a long time, too.

Epilogue

Her fingers trailed along the spines of books, lazily looking at the titles, not really searching for anything in particular but observing all the same.

It was simply a way of passing the time.

What little there was of it remaining.

Word had come to them a week ago that they were needed back in England, and to return there at their earliest convenience.

Hal hadn't been entirely pleased by the return command, not after the blessed time she'd been having with her husband once they'd sent the information back. Everything was wonderful, magical, and utterly beautiful in this time and space, and returning to the drudgery of their lives would end it all.

Well, not all of it. She would keep her husband, after all.

There was something to be said for that.

Still, she'd put up a decent fight over remaining.

"But there's more we could do!" she'd protested when John had brought back word from Ruse that they were being sent home. "There's so much we don't know! So much we could still uncover for them!"

"I know that," John had told her, his voice soothing, as always. "Ruse knows that, too. No doubt the Shopkeepers are aware, as well. Our task was to open the door here. Now it is open."

Hal scowled up at him. "Can we close it again? Just for a bit longer?"

Her husband had cupped her cheek, stroking her skin softly. "This isn't our country, *Ange*. We have no authority, so there is nothing else we can do. As operatives, we must obey orders."

She hadn't liked that answer, but it wasn't her husband's fault that it was the truth.

"Besides," he'd added, "when we return to London, we may actually continue that dance we never finished."

Her cheeks flamed in response, and she'd put up no further protests.

Then, he had surprised her in the sweetest way by showing her the response he'd sent to Weaver.

Will return to England once my wife and I have enjoyed our wedded bliss a few days more. We look forward to the debriefing upon our return.

She'd taken great pains to thank him appropriately for that, and he'd made it clear he appreciated the gesture.

But now, all of that had passed, and they could not in good conscience remain in Paris longer. Her relations were sorry to lose them, and the children were distraught to lose their favorite imaginary *chien*. They were all invited to visit them as soon as they were situated in their new house in London, which had cheered many of them.

There had been a lengthy discussion before bed that evening about the aforementioned new house in London, and nothing was quite settled yet. But if Hal knew her godfather, and she flattered herself that she did, he would already have a house in mind for them. One endowed with all the protections he would see fit to impose upon his goddaughter and the man he had entrusted her to.

And then there would be Thad to contend with.

He would remain with them, of course, as he had sworn to do, but there was some debate as to what capacity he might serve in.

That, too, had not been settled yet.

But in time, it would be. It all would be.

"Saying farewell?"

Hal smiled and turned to face the door, placing her back against the shelves of books. "In a way. I never did spend much time in here, and it seems a shame."

John smiled at her, the affection plain for anyone to see. "You said you were not much of a reader."

"If I found something that I might enjoy reading, I could be a reader," she informed him with a sniff. "You never know."

"No, I suppose I don't." He sighed and looked around the ostentatious library, shaking his head. "I don't know how, but I think I may actually miss this finery."

Hal giggled, though she understood all the same. "It does grow on you. Perhaps we may have some fine things in our home in London."

His smile deepened, as it usually did when she referred to anything regarding their marriage. "Perhaps we might."

She clasped her hands before her, tilting her head back to look up at the painting above them. "Is it time to leave, then?"

"Shortly," John replied, coming further into the room. "They're loading up the coach now, and Jean is sending us home with a good stock of French brandy. Says he'll give us a letter for the examiners that will ensure that we have no trouble getting it home."

Hal barked a loud laugh. "Why do I have no doubt of that?" She lowered her eyes to her husband, now more directly before her. "He told me to come in here and find a book or two to take with me. He doesn't know what they have here, as he rarely comes in anymore. Apparently, René is the reader, not Jean."

"Well, René is a romantic," John reminded her. "He's the reader, he's the opera lover, he's the poet… Bit of a popinjay, really."

Coughing in surprise, Hal flicked her hand to smack her husband in the chest. "He is not!"

John's expression turned so sardonic Hal began to laugh uproariously. "The man is a puppy, *Ange*, and a sycophant. I daresay if we had more wealth, he would have introduced us to everyone of his acquaintance, flattered us endlessly, and never let us walk or breathe unless he was there to see to our every need."

"You're ridiculous." Hal shook her head, returning her attention to the books. "I presume all of your extended relations are perfectly rational and well-behaved?"

"So, what books do you think you'll be taking with us?" he asked at once, suddenly quite interested in the books at hand. "Anything striking your fancy?"

Hal snorted and turned around to kiss her husband once.

"Excellent transition, my love. So subtle."

"Your attentions to my improvement are much appreciated," he replied cheekily, "as always."

Rolling her eyes, she turned back around and wandered along the row of books. "To answer your question, I'm not sure. He mentioned a book or two my mother might have had that are still here somewhere, but he couldn't think which ones."

"That would be a treasure, to be sure." John took her hand and began to search the books with her, sharing her newfound appreciation for her mother, now that she had told him of Skean's revelations regarding her. "Any thoughts?"

"Not really," Hal sighed. "She wasn't much of a reader when I was a child. At least, not that I saw."

Hand in hand, they scanned the shelves, fingers occasionally stroking against each other's in a warm familiarity that was becoming so natural.

Marriage was a funny business, and loving whom one married was even more peculiar.

"Oh my," John suddenly said, amusement rife in his tone. "That's something I didn't expect to see on these shelves."

"What is it?" Hal came to him, looking where he pointed. She laughed once. "Mary Wollstonecraft?"

"A Vindication for the Rights of Women," John read. "And they have A Vindication for the Rights of Men, as well. In fact, they have several Mary Wollstonecraft works. Impressive."

Hal eyed the works surrounding them and pointed one shelf lower. "Look here. *The Rights of Man* by Paine. Oof." She shook her head. "I couldn't make it through that one. Too scholarly."

"See here," John murmured as though he hadn't heard. "*Du contrat social; ou Principes du droit politique.*" He gave her a strange look. "Rousseau."

That wasn't a standard work to be kept in one's residential library, to be sure. Hal looked again. "And another Rousseau. *Discours sur l'origine et les fondements de l'inégalité parmi les hommes.*"

"*Ange.*"

Hal's eyes flicked to John's hands, holding a pamphlet he'd pulled from the shelf. "*Qu'est-ce que le tiers-état?*" she read. Then her heart leapt to her throat, and she met her husband's eyes. "Sieyès."

They shared horrified looks, not that Sieyès's work ought to horrify, only his significance to the Faction. Combined with the other works sitting in this library at the moment, the coincidence was too great.

"Could it be?" Hal breathed, her hands beginning to tremble. "René?"

John shook his head in disbelief, though not, she noticed, in denial. He scanned the shelves around them, then pulled one book out.

A history of the revolution of France.

He opened the book to discover that it was a false book, hollowed out to be nothing more than a box among books, hidden in plain sight.

Glancing at the slightly open but empty doorway, Hal huddled close to her husband to pull out the documents stashed within the box.

Lists of names were among the papers, each with dates by them. Some were from the days of the Revolution; some were as early as the week before. A few names, she noticed, had been crossed out. Most, however, were not.

There were at least fifty names there, and all of them French. And each of them had tally marks beside their names, though there was no indication what any of it meant.

Hal took the box and rifled through other papers within, her heart sinking with dread. Maps of London, names of important figures in both Society and government, and a few names of known Faction supporters on English soil were among them. This was far too organized to be anything less than what it appeared. But how could he be one of them? He hadn't been at the meeting, and he'd been at the ball with them…

John pulled out a folded document and opened it carefully. Hal nearly dropped the box when she saw it in full.

A map of England with several stretches of coastline in Kent, Essex, and Sussex marked.

Most of the marks, however, were in Kent.

The coastline of Kent.

Hal looked at John again, the color draining from both of their faces. There was only one thing they could do at this point, only one course of action.

She managed a very weak, very hard swallow. "We have to warn the Convent."

Coming Soon

Fortune Favors the Sparrow

Agents of the Convent
Book One

"Some new mischief this way comes."

by

Rebecca Connolly

Also from Phase Publishing

Emily Daniels:

Devlin's Daughter
Lucia's Lament
A Song for a Soldier

Grace Donovan:

Saint's Ride

Laura Beers:

Saving Shadow
A Peculiar Courtship
To Love a Spy

Tiffany Dominguez:

The Eidolon

Ferrell Hornsby:

If We're Breathing, We're Serving

Printed in the USA
CPSIA information can be obtained
at www.ICGtesting.com
LVHW021541311023
762557LV00004B/447